MW00441130

THE LIGHTHOUSE GHOST
of Yaquina Bay

Alexandra Mason

Chapters 1, 7, and 8 first appeared in
"Tuesday," 10 (2016), 35-45
Chapter 1 was read on KYAQ radio
November 22, 2016
Chapter 8 appeared on "The Creative Café" website, June
20, 2017

©2017 by the author
ISBN 10- 0911443495
13-978-0911443493
Lincoln County Historical Society
Newport, Oregon
Do not duplicate without express permission
Cover art and illustrations by Lila Pasarelli

For my sister Karen
(1942-2017)

This novel came entirely from my imagination. The kernel of the narrative, including the names of some of the characters, I found in another work of fiction, "The Haunted Light at Newport by the Sea," by Lischen M. Miller, published in 1899. I have taken the liberty of including the local color of places that exist and that I know in Newport, Oregon. While I hope my novel will encourage the reader's own imagination, be assured that these events did not actually occur. If the reader visits the lighthouse or the cemetery or other places mentioned, please take no liberties based on the reading of this little novel. Ghosts do live vibrantly in our minds, and we should let them exist in that space only.

Newport's Bayfront

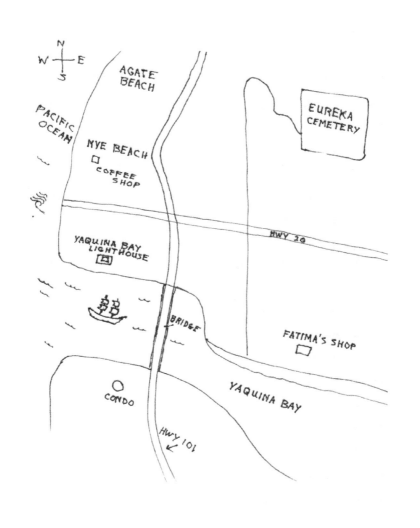

1— Muriel

Dark again, always dark, and the air so moist the boundaries of her own body began to blur into mist. Muriel felt around her. Hard walls with square edges—she must be inside the house. The dampness had done its work on any source of escape from the lightkeeper's abandoned dwelling. Although the kitchen lock held a key, it had long since rusted into disuse, and someone, apparently trying to force the lock open, had snapped off the key, forever closing the lock. The front door held no key, but its lock too was completely rusted. Had someone tried to rescue her, the door must needs be stormed in.

No other egress seemed possible. From outside and below the house loomed much larger than actuality. The first floor contained the small kitchen and study to the back. The front of the house held the dining room and sitting room. These four chambers surrounded a large central hallway with the solid staircase up to the second floor. Even from the entry one could glance up and see the helix of the second flight, thirteen steps leading to the door to the lighthouse tower. Four squarely-placed bedrooms marked the corners of the second floor. Their windows bore no greater hope for escape. Someone had secured all the shutters, perhaps against an onshore wind, and the damp years had rendered them closed permanently. No one in this now growing coastal community except the occasional thrillseeker paid mind to the old house and tower. It was an oddity, to be visited as a tourist attraction and harrumphed at.

As she had night after night for an eternity it seemed, Muriel could only enact her scene of hope. Pressing against the wall of the squarely-built staircase with one hand and carefully lifting her skirts with the other, she scaled its risers. Only sixteen steps to the top, she thought, counting each one. Then three steps across the landing and the climb was circular, up the helical staircase leading to the door to the tower and the crowning light. Undeterred by its years of darkness in dereliction, Muriel had scavenged from the rest of the house flint and lanterns, tapers, extra wax and oil, anything that would fuel a small flicker of hope. These she rationed, allowing herself to burn her signal light only to the count of one hundred each time.

Were that especial sloop close enough to shore in the vast Pacific, with its swarthy, beetle-browed captain searching for his shanghaied wife, perchance he might espy this dim beacon and remember also his beautiful genteel daughter, left at Newport for a rest from the churning of the waves—she, Muriel Trevenard, now as lost to him as his beloved spouse.

As Muriel reached the lighthouse crown, she could see the floating illuminations far out there in the sea, like opals in a giant tiara. Tonight the fog was only just beginning to rise, not yet enshrouding her spot of vigil in murky nothingness, turning it into the loneliest place in the world. Which was worse she could not decide: merely imagining that her father's sloop was readying to cross the bar in the great whiteness or seeing those ghostly lights clearly but so far away. Faced with these two painful alternatives, she often let out an involuntary moan of anguish. If any light neared the tower, by either land or sea, in her excitement she would cry out "Help me! Help me! Help me!" in frenzy, always three times, until her breath and hope left her un-befriended and solitary once again.

On this night she trimmed her lantern and began her count, looking wistfully at the floating opals of light. As she neared fifty in her count to one hundred, she turned her gaze across the harbor's entrance and across the bay. What had once been nothing but a rocky shore now held buildings of some sort, and from one of these Muriel made out a small light like hers, wanly seeking a reply, she imagined. As she sighed, it seemed her involuntary moan could wake somebody—whom? The living?

2—HAL

As he admired the sleek dolphin shape of the blown-glass lamp, Hal was mystified. Yet again tonight he could sleep only fitfully, here in the paradise of the Oregon coast in an exquisitely fitted out condo, on what was to be a restful and healing vacation with his daughter. So often lately he woke suddenly at 3 a.m. with even his open eyes retaining the image of a pale female face floating before him. The apparition was no one he recognized. At first he thought he might be hallucinating the image of his late wife. So vital as a person and to his life, she had been diagnosed with colon cancer and declined with heart-wrenching haste—his only solace being the short time she had suffered before dying.

While Hal presented a stoical face to the world—in part to be an anchor for his fourteen-year-old daughter Amelia—he felt his insides filled as with pieces of broken glass. There were shards of strength, slivers of joyful remembrance, and broken bits of a fully loving husband and father in him, but these all had shredded his heart into a frantic loneliness and despair. Hal no longer felt a direction to his life. Amelia notwithstanding, he was no longer glad to greet a new day. For her, he could contrive daily events—nature walks in the estuaries or crabbing in the bay, a picnic on the beach or a whale-watch cruise—but he could find no joy for himself. Numbly and gamely he went through the motions, but the blank space Gillian's passing had left in him threatened to shroud him in an eternal darkness.

He had always dived into his work as a microbiologist with anticipation, loving to observe the very basis of life—those molecules of helical DNA—and becoming fascinated with discovering hidden links. Why did we respond to the whale's song? Because it vibrated our strands of commonality. Why were we fixated on the tide? Because its primordial soup was also in our blood. Why must we collect and inspect shells? Because they are the abodes of our ancestors.

These webs of connectedness had always sustained him, giving his life a purpose and meaning far beyond its small personal events. But now his mind's eye had turned inward, and he could perceive only the vast and empty darkness of his loss.

In the foggy dark of a Newport night Hal despaired of becoming whole. He ran the old metaphors through his mind: yes, his heart felt literally broken, in shards, barely able to keep him alive. He recalled the story told by Aristophanes in Plato's "Symposium," about how originally people were perfectly round and rolled so successfully all about Earth that the gods decided to hinder their progress by splitting the human globes in half. Tonight Hal felt all angles, and the points were piercing him, torturing his insides. He had lost his half and wobbled about incomplete.

Hal knew he had descended from hardy stock and hoped he might find unknown reserves of inner strength. His colleagues at the lab had urged him to get away to the coast he loved. Perhaps here he could regain his spirit of hope and his passion for inquiry. They missed the old Hal, who inspired their work and their lives too. For at least three generations he could trace his forebears back in Newport, on his father's side. One ancestor had been a fisherman and another a harbor-master. Perhaps this was why Hal felt the pull of the sea so intensely. Since those were the days before the opening to Yaquina Bay was widened and calmed by jetties, this now placid harbor where the river met the Pacific would have posed more of a challenge—and a danger.

Absent-mindedly running his hand down the glossy sides of the dolphin-lamp now dimly lighting the room, Hal gazed at the bay and tried to imagine it untamed as in the past. The now-defunct lighthouse would have been vital then to mark the entrance to the bay. Isolated and abandoned, it sat across from him, on the north side just seaward of the bridge. It was cloudy tonight and the mist was rising, but as Hal bent forward to douse his light, his eye caught a glimmer out there in the gloom. Shaking his head to clear it of his wool-gathering, he thought, *now I've even imagined the lighthouse at work again. First a floating face, and then a phantom light—I need to get a grip*, the scientist in him said. Before turning back to the bedroom, he checked again: there was no longer an answering light.

3—Amelia

"R U misn me." Lying awake in a bed shaped like a boat, its sails fashioned into a sort of canopy, Amelia vainly composed text messages she *would* be sending if Daddy—or Pah-rent, as she called him—had not confiscated her cell phone. Of course she was devastated by the loss of her mother, but she had put this sadness into one secret place inside her, and as the weeks passed it became a less palpable throb. Why, when all the other kids were spending their summer working on a Habitat for Humanity house, did Pah-rent think it would be better for the two of them to "get away" together? Amelia had no urge to get away from life; she wanted to get on with it, jump into it. She did love the coast, but there was a limit to her enjoyment of Daddy's contrived little-kid activities.

She knew he was hurting inside, although he pretended everything was normal. She also knew he needed her right now, as the image of her mother and the only family he had left. So she played along at building sand castles and picking up agates. At least some days when it was sunny, she could work on her tan.

But think of what she was missing back home in Salem. All the best kids from middle school were working on the house project—girls and boys, too. She could be wearing cute cut-offs and flirting with Tom as they measured planks and pounded nails. She could be giggling with her friends as they watched the boys try to prove their manly strength. Pah-rent had taken her phone because he knew she would be unable to resist constant contact with them.

He wanted her to "slow down" and relax. "You can write them all long letters while we sit on the beach," he said. What century was *he* from?

Probably the worst part was that when she returned in fall, her group would all have this common experience, and it would be like in-jokes for them. Although she knew they would accept her back in, she would feel like an outsider. All the college-prep kids would have shared the events of a summer she lacked. New bonds would be formed, but Amelia would have to pick up where she had left off. What new flirtations would Tom have? What might have caught his eye during the summer? And she couldn't even find that out until September because she was sure none of her friends would be sending *her* long letters! IM-ing was much more their style.

She reminded herself to bug Pah-rent about the phone again tomorrow. He had a goofy clambake planned for them. Well, maybe it would rain—if tonight's fog was any indication. Throwing back the nautical coverlet, Amelia sighed deeply. Lately she woke up in the middle of the night, not so much missing her mother as worrying about Pah-rent. What could she do to help him get back to his old self? When they went for a cruise or walked on the beach, he just seemed distant, even other-worldly. She wished they could make some friends—or find some kind of project to investigate. Pah-rent always loved the challenge of a mystery.

Her beachy room offered little in the way of late-night distraction. Pah-rent had removed all the TVs too, so they would not be tempted to stay in the condo and veg out. From an early age she had loved to sketch, especially the faces of people she met, and her drawing pad was filled with half-finished portraits of her friends. Paging though the pad now made her lonely and homesick. She paused to add more detail to Tom's face, and that made her even more sure that she was missing out on some important adventures back home. She laid the pad aside, and her eyes scanned the strange room.

At the foot of her boat-bed there was one bookcase, in what looked like a shipping trunk or treasure chest. Lifting its lid, Amelia sorted through—Anne Morrow Lindbergh's "A Gift from the Sea," James Patterson's "The Beach House," Ron Lovell's "Murder at Yaquina Head." All of these seemed awfully adult and just like what you'd read on vacation. At the bottom of the chest was one last small brownish book, stained with age. Amelia read its title, "The Haunted Light at Newport by the Sea," by Lischen M. Miller, 1899. Now *here* might be a mystery worthy of Pah-rent.

4—HAL

Hoping the aroma of bacon frying would pull Amelia from her room, Hal gently blended the pancake batter. Because of his interrupted night's sleep, he had risen later than usual. His daughter seemed tacitly on the same schedule, although he was unaware of her reason for lying abed. Her delay in joining him allowed him to gather his thoughts about last night and regroup for the day, which would need a change in plans since the mist had become a steady drizzle. No clambake today.

Hal took a long draw on his coffee—made from the best beans ever, he thought, obtained from the Espressgo stand on the highway south of the bridge. Mentally he constructed a list of activities suitably edifying for a father-daughter combo. There was the aquarium. Keiko, the famous killer whale, was no longer there or even on this earth, but his enormous pool had been refashioned into a walk-through shark tank. Because Hal was also a marine biologist, he would have open access to the Marine

Science Center as well. As a surprise for Amelia, he had arranged for a special tour of the facilities, followed by a whale-spotting tour, but today was too gloomy and inclement for that trip.

Turning the bacon and glancing out the window, Hal flashed on last night's visions—first, of the woman's pale face that had floated in the air, and then of the soft light he had seen in the tower of the lighthouse—seen, or imagined. The floating face he dare not try to understand. Since Gillian's death he had experienced a variety of unsettling dreams. Often the two of them were happily reliving events from their life together. They would be cooking dinner or hiking through the woods or driving on a country road, just "being here now" as the saying goes. Eventually these dreams would take an ugly turn, always some variation of entrapment. A dis-embodied head, however, was new to his night stories. The scientist in him made a mental note to look for that dim light again tonight. He needed to amass some empirical data, or perhaps just sign in to the loony bin!

He could hear Amelia showering now. After removing the bacon to drain on paper towels, he refilled his cup and sat at the table—fashioned to look like a huge spool of boat-rigging rope—to scan the brochures describing area sights. Nature walk at Yaquina Head—not in this rain. Sea Lion Caves—just too drippy today. Outlet mall shopping and beach curio shopping—not his idea of vacation fare. Yaquina Bay Lighthouse—the source of his hallucination, just across the bay! Out of an intense curiosity, he would see if this might interest his increasingly sophisticated daughter.

Getting her to think about Newport's history might keep her from obsessing about what fun her friends were having at home. He knew Amelia had a strong and curious mind. It just needed direction and encouragement. He would remind her that this might be the lighthouse that had guided one of her great-great-grandfathers back to safety in the bay. He would try to get her to feel the pull of the tides in her blood, too.

Here came his shiny daughter now, and Hal jumped up to pour the pancakes onto the griddle.

5—Amelia

"Hello, sleepyhead," her father sang out as Amelia's stomach responded to the rich aromas of the kitchenette. "I guess this sea air is helping you get the rest you need!" he added.

Amelia noted that he was wearing his game face today, pretending to be cheerful and carefree.

"That nautical bed must be pretty comfy," he said as he flipped the pancakes. "Grab the syrup, would you, honey? It's nearly soup."

This was Pah-rent's way of saying the pancakes were ready—the unasked question was supposedly "Is it soup yet?" Suppressing a groan at his corniness, Amelia deposited the book she was carrying onto the table and went to the pantry. She returned with the syrup just as he set their full plates on the dinette table.

"Mmm—smells great, Dad!"

He smiled with gratitude and began with a sigh, "I know this will be a disappointment to you, but today's clambake will be called off because of the rain. Let's find something fun we can do indoors. You know, I was thinking we should go over to the Yaquina Bay Lighthouse. We've been staring at it for days, taking its presence for granted. You remember, don't you, that your great-great-great-grandfather worked as a fisherman out of this harbor? He might have been guided safely home by that very light. I think we owe it to our family history to get acquainted with that place, don't you?"

Amelia kept chewing. She really wouldn't need that much convincing in this matter. The little book she had found in the chest had been a quick read, and she had been unable to shake the story from her mind the rest of the night.

Over a century ago the lighthouse had drawn kids her own age to explore its mysteries, and there'd been a tragic occurrence. So what if it was back in the dark ages? She could easily relate to the antics of a group of teenagers roaming the beach and out for a lark. Her curiosity about the lighthouse was already piqued, but she let Pah-rent continue with his cajoling of her. He would feel victorious if he felt he had sold her on this idea.

"There's a house attached to the light," he continued. "Actually, the light is in the upper part of the house, very unusual. The keeper could live right there and just walk upstairs to tend the light. So not only can we learn about the signaling function, but we can see how folks lived back in the 1800s. I hear they've restored the house nearly to its original condition."

Amelia was enjoying his effort to win her over.

Feigning lack of interest, she said, "Hmmm. Is there any juice?"

"Yes, in the door of the fridge. How about some more bacon? So what do you say to the lighthouse? Doesn't it sound fascinating? If you're feeling hardy today we can put on our rain gear and walk over the bridge."

Amelia tortured him just a bit longer with her silence. This was getting rich. Dad was so enthusiastic, so nerdy, and so predictable.

"Well, honey, I don't think anybody is living there now, but here's something strange for you," Dad continued. "Last night I thought I saw a light— or, more exactly, a pale version of *the* light coming from the tower. Maybe I was just sort of dreaming. When I looked again it was gone. We can ask them today what that could have been. There must be an explanation—or else I'm seeing ghosts!"

6—HAL

Amelia was having a sudden fit of coughing. Lifting her arm above her head and thumping her on the back, Hal tried to help his daughter clear her windpipe.

"Honey, are you all right now?"

The reactions of his teenaged daughter were often surprising and perplexing. This morning she had gone from remote lack of interest to an intense physical response. What had he said to set her off?

Blowing her nose on her napkin, Amelia looked at him with wide eyes.

"Dad. Don't you know the story? It was in my room, hidden at the bottom of this treasure chest—this funky old book—look, here it is—I couldn't sleep, and there was no TV, and I was just looking for anything—well, a bunch of kids were picnicking and no one lived in the lighthouse, and they went in to check it out, and this one girl forgot her handkerchief and went back in, and Dad, they never saw her again!"

Amelia stopped to catch her breath. It had been a long while since Hal had experienced such energy and animation in his daughter. She had even called him "Dad" instead of her hip term, "Pah-rent." He could understand why this story had worked its way under her skin—a teenaged girl as a victim, and a band of kids exploring. Freedom, community, and melodramatic romance all in a single package.

"Ah, yes, I vaguely recall a legend, now that you mention it. It's been years since I thought about it. Let's see, the girl was some kind of orphan, wasn't she?"

If he could build on Amelia's initial attraction to this story, he might get her absorbed in a history project. The lighthouse tale might fork off into a genealogical study, and looking into the history of their forebears in Newport might bond them together, occupying them even on the rainiest of summer days. Then on the clear days there might be sites to hunt down, spots where ancestors might have lived or roads they might have traversed. Hal thought this might actually be the key to a successful summer with his daughter.

"No, she wasn't an *orphan*. Just like us, she had only her male Pah-rent. They sailed around together looking for the mother. The pirates had taken her! The dad dropped this girl—Muriel was her name— off for the summer in Newport while he did some intensive searching. This guy named Harold had it bad for Muriel, and their clique liked to prowl around town and on the beach. Nobody was living in the lighthouse then, so they all went in to look around. And you know what they found?"

Amelia's eyes were completely dilated.

Playing along, he said, "A bloody ghost in chains?"

"No! Even worse! They found a secret door near the lighthouse stairs. It was so dark that nobody could tell what was behind it. But when Muriel went back inside to get her hanky she had dropped, something got her, Dad. They found blood by that door, but no Muriel."

"Hmm," Hal mused, pretending to take this all seriously. "I think maybe that lighthouse is too scary and dangerous for *us* to visit. I wouldn't want to lose my favorite daughter to the menace of the tower. What do you say we hit the art gallery instead?"

"Da-ad!"

She was so intrigued with the legend that she'd gone genuine, forgetting again to call him Pah-rent. He was in support of anything that would curb his daughter's teenage boredom and cynicism.

"All right, then, let's get over there and meet some ghosts!" he teased.

After piling the dishes in the sink and wiping off the stove and table, Hal rummaged around in their pile of outdoor gear. He handed up waterproof macintoshes with hoods, and they struggled into them, snapping and zipping and velcroing every fastener tight. They resembled giant amoebas—a large green blob and his smaller companion.

Today's rain was more like a fine mist. In his mind Hal ran through words from his Oregon vocabulary that might accurately describe it. Let's see: definitely not spitting, pelting, bucketing, lashing, or downpouring. It wasn't a sprinkle or even a drizzle, for it didn't seem to be coming down; it simply surrounded you in fine wetness. No drops were visible. But it wasn't quite dense enough to be fog, either. There was still fairly good visibility through the mist cloud.

As they left the condo, Hal glanced across the Yaquina River, widened out here into the broad bay that opened into the grand Pacific. Their destination, the squat house now bereft of its oil-fueled Fresnel lens, which had been moved to the Yerba Buena lighthouse, still bore its square tower rising from the second story, and it sat placidly in the mist. The light had been operative only for three years in the 1870s. But the house, now 140 years old, was well preserved, and it seemed to survey and guard this entrance to Newport and, further upriver, Toledo.

They'd need to circle up to the bridge, seemingly just at their right hand as they faced the bay, traverse its span of three-fifths of a mile, then circle west again to the lighthouse. It was a longer walk than it appeared to the eye, and in this mist as well, but he was fit and Amelia was young. This bridge, like many along the Oregon coast, was a magnificent monument to art deco and the Roosevelt years. It had been constructed between 1934 and 1936 as part of the Works Project Administration, and it had been designed by Conde

B. McCullough with a grand arching shape flanked on either end by concrete obelisks.

As they walked he began humming and then said, "Amelia, come on, sing with me. . . . 'I love to go a-wandering, my knapsack on my back.' One step to each beat. It's a roving song."

Amelia groaned at his corny enthusiasm, but as they labored up the incline to the center of the bridge, she began to shout with him, "Val-der-ree! Val-der-rah!"

No mountains here to supply an echo, but they were invigorated by exercise, the cool air, and the vast expanse of reflective water. Just as they reached "Val-der-rah-ha-ha-ha-ha-ha" and the center of the bridge, Hal glanced up from the hood of his mac. His eye had caught movement to the west. Just entering the jaw of the two jetties and emerging from the mist was a tall ship with sails fully unfurled and filled with the wind, coming into the harbor. What a breath-taking sight, and they were perfectly positioned to catch the full effect.

Hal touched Amelia's arm, and she peered out from the hood of her mac—then drew in her breath. The sight did seem magical.

"It's a pirate ship!" she exclaimed.

They leaned on the railing at the center of the bridge and watched as the magnificent *Hawaiian Chieftain* glided silently toward them and then underneath them. As it passed below they could see the cannons on deck and a crew in nineteenth-century garb bustling about.

Suddenly their day seemed charmed, and both became light-hearted. They were like partners in a happy conspiracy. As they began the incline down to the north end of the bridge, this time it was Amelia herself who began the refrain, "Val-der-rah-ha-ha-ha-ha!"

7—MURIEL

By day she generally retreated to the closet on the upper landing, the room with iron walls into which she had once, while still quick, disappeared. The house had been turned into a museum of sorts and tourists tramped through the halls and rooms all day. Children shouted and ran rambunctiously up and down the main staircase. They had painted over the iron door so it looked like an ordinary wall. Although no one could see her, she found their movements unsettling. She might be able to glide invisibly past them, but their energy was disturbing in general. It served no useful function for her to wander among them. She found it safer and more comfortable to tuck herself away for the duration.

The disappearance of the iron door behind which she rested served to protect her from tourists as well. While her imprisonment in the lighthouse was bleak and endless, it was not always solitary. On occasion during her nocturnal ramblings she would encounter another entrapped soul, a wraith wandering as she did. She had her mission to ignite her candle as a signal to her father's ship. She awaited his return, and his rescue of her. Even if he were altered by his journey after all the decades, searching for her shanghaied mother, she could always recognize him by the big scar running across the left side of his face from ear to nose.

Aside from the return of her sea-faring father and his release of her from this lighthouse prison, her future seemed hopeless and eternally the same. She hid by day in the iron-clad cupboard. She wandered by night, performing her candle ritual with a decreasing glimmer of expectation.

At times she had attempted making connection with the living who walked through this house, but they did not seem to notice. Similarly, the others— she was reluctant to call them ghosts, like her, for she still felt like an intact individual consciousness— they seemed trance-like, intent on their own missions, whatever those might be. Sometimes they had crossed paths silently on the staircases, eyes forward and focused on a distant goal.

How could anyone, living or dead, help her anyway? Even if she could somehow be released from this lighthouse prison, then what? She had no other place to go. Her father would still be away on the open sea, and the young man Harold who'd brought her here surely no longer trod the earth. Precisely how long she'd wandered these halls and rooms she could not say. At first she'd scratched a mark on the wall for each night she lit the candle. But soon enough marks filled the entire space. She tried cross hatching existing marks until they were all X-ed over, and then she X-ed from left to right on top of those. Long since she'd abandoned that attempt to keep track of time when the wall no longer bore any paint, simply a blur of starry scratches indicating decades past.

But today she felt an unusual sense of excitement, even expectancy. She dared not call it hope. Something about that glimmer of light she'd seen across the bay last night seemed like a new connection with this current world. It held people and activity—which until now had seemed separate from her and irrelevant to rescue from her plight. But that feeble light had spoken to her as another searching soul. It had beamed back as if in answer to her.

With a maximum exertion of energy and will, she was able to materialize briefly to the living. Was there someone out there who might become her ally if she could make herself known? If, as she had begun at last to fear, her father could no longer return to rescue her, what escape might there be from this perpetual sameness, this endless loneliness trapped in the abandoned lighthouse? Her imagination faltered at visualizing the actual possibilities, yet some part of her clung to a hope. If the opportunity presented itself, she was ready to fling herself forward in an attempt to traverse that tenuous border between the two dimensions.

During her decades of wandering the house she had tried any option for escape that presented itself. Desperation had led her to a strange discovery. One evening before the trees had grown so tall she had gazed absently from an upstairs window and focused her will on a walker passing by. This man seemed to be enjoying the dying light and the bay water lapping at his path, and his eyes looked toward the sea. Something about his frame and his gait made her think of her sea-captain father, and for an instant she thought he'd found her.

As her heart quickened, she willed him to come toward the lighthouse, willed him to look up and see her, still awaiting his return. And the man did just that, almost simultaneous with her wish. He paused and peered toward her for only a moment, but in that moment she realized her power. She could affect the living. She still had the force of her worldly self.

But how this might avail her was doubtful. What help there might be for her was meager, and what might she offer the living except for a sad report on this limbo of an afterlife? She was unsure how she might recognize such a living soul to reach out to. The faces of those who traipsed past her hiding place day after endless day seemed of a sameness to her. These modern folk appeared casual and unserious. How would one of them respond to her materializing? She could imagine an ado of shrill screams. No doubt they would fear her as the unknown, the uncontrollable.

And those screams would vibrate through her own soul, unsettling its will to be substantial. Ironic in a way, how her well-being still might depend on the realities of this living middle earth. She felt the surge of will for some sort of heroic action, if not to save or rescue herself, at least to catalyze a change. Her endless ritual of sending out the light had borne no results. She struggled to keep hold of a sense of time passing, the hatchmarks in the tower a testament to that effort. Within the misty haze of her daily activity she found time elusive.

But being in time perhaps was the key difference between those in her state and the yet living. They scurried about less aimlessly, with an apparent sense of direct action followed by result. They seemed to know where they were headed and what came next. She envied this resolution, even if its practitioners were unmindful of their regimen. In the stories of their lives time marched boldly through every episode, leading toward a certain end. In a sense she'd already reached her own end, untimely as it had come, yet here she bided, hoping for an epilogue as she gazed across the bay. The glimmer of an answering light might be the omen for the concluding chapter of her death.

8—MURIEL

Peering idly out the front bedroom window, she was glad she'd relocated from the closet. A few tourists wandered through the room around her, but they were of the quiet kind, and they did not deplete her own spiritual energy. Outside the house on the path along the bay and down to the beach she saw living folks strolling along. They laughed with each other as they walked and talked, and her mind returned to that fateful day she became trapped here in the lighthouse.

Like those groups she now observed, she and her friends had frolicked along the beach that day so long ago. Light-heartedly they had played a sort of tag as they moved along. Harold had singled her out for extra attention, and as she dodged his advances she could feel the weight of the small shells she'd found on the sand and placed in her pocket alongside her handkerchief. Now, absent-mindedly, her hand returned to her overskirt pocket—it was missing the shells and linen, but she still felt a few grains of sand along the seamed edges.

Being with friends her own age had lessened her concerned longing for her father, at least temporarily. That had been a happy and carefree summer, a welcome respite from the constant rolling of the waves. On the ship she'd always felt a bit ill at ease, unsteady on her feet and upset at stomach. And nothing compared to the stark and blank vista of the open sea with no land in sight, unless it was the uncertainty and apparent endlessness of her present state.

She had been unclear about her father's plan in their quest for her lost mother. Her kid-napping had been so strange. *En route* to Newport to visit old friends, the ship had stopped in San Francisco for provisions. She and her mother had gone to a supper house while her father handled business matters. When her mother failed to return from the outhouse, Muriel had alerted the staff, who announced that marauding troops of pirates were out to shanghai any able body here on shore, male and female alike. They would put their kidnapped victims to work on their ship—or to other even more unthinkable uses.

She'd not seen her father as alarmed as he was when he heard the news. He'd immediately trundled her onto the ship, and off they set, looking for that pirate vessel and her mother.

What would they do if they found the ship? She could not even imagine a cannon battle, yet how else could they rescue her mother? Perhaps her father planned a silent night approach. He could stealthily board the ship and locate his wife, unless they were discovered. In that case poor Muriel would be without both her parents—a situation that might equal her current state of . . . misplacement.

Mentally she clung to what she had known, her father and their need to reunite their family. Anything else was a frightening unknown, and she dreaded to consider the possibilities. Indeed, what was she now? She was aware that her accustomed life as a teen-age girl had been taken away. Her mind shrank from calling this "death." Aside from her entrapment within this lighthouse, she felt much the same as before—just unspeakably lonely and lost.

She had returned to the house that day to retrieve her handkerchief, inadvertently dropped as they had explored all the crannies of this place that now she knew so well. The empty structure had not intimidated her. She re-entered and quickly made her way to the top of the central stairs, certain that she would complete her mission and soon rejoin her gang of friends. On up the spiral stairs toward the tower, and there the handkerchief lay, near the strange iron door. All of her friends had been mystified by this unusual portal strangely placed here on the upper landing, but no one was brave enough to open it and peer inside. What did they expect to reside within? Ghosts? Skeletons? Even on a dare the manly Harold had shrunk from the task.

She stooped to pick up her handkerchief and turned to descend the stairs, but a small scraping sound arrested her. It seemed to come from behind the mysterious door, and her curiosity took her over completely. Perhaps she could be the one to discover the secret of the iron door and what lay behind it.

Then she could tease Harold mercilessly for his reticence. It would be a humorous moment, to be sure, and it would make for good flirting. Muriel examined the door closely and found a sliding latch. She lifted its knob and exerted pressure, but it seemed stuck—perhaps from disuse—and in need of oil. She pushed harder, and it released with a jolt, slitting the side of her finger in the process.

By reflex she put the wound to her mouth, then looked at it closely. It was definitely bleeding—and throbbing. *Drat*, she thought, and wrapped the handkerchief, which she still held, around the cut. But her curiosity drove her on. Balling her hand into a fist, she had opened the door with her other hand and stepped into a small closet, noticeably cooler than the house itself. The space was small, and she had to crouch down. She was startled by a mouse scurrying away through a tiny opening. Feeling along the sides of the dim space, she found slits from which came a whooshing sound like the tide—interspersed with a low moan.

Her mind whirled with questions and possibilities. Was this a cooling chamber for storing foodstuffs and perishables? If so, why so far from the kitchen? Or was it some sort of tunnel or passageway? At first the moan alarmed her, but she realized it must be the wind. Somehow this closet seemed open to the elements below, the sea and the air. Testing the slitted wall by rattling it, she thought it loosened, and she extended her wounded hand to steady herself on the iron door itself. In an instant the wall gave way, the handkerchief dropped from her bleeding hand near the opening, the door snapped shut, and she felt herself dropping into a cool expanse of nothingness.

———————

When she came to from what seemed like a blackout, she was lying next to the closed iron door. Drops of blood spotted the floor near her, and her bloody handkerchief lay next to her hand—now no longer throbbing, or bleeding.

Muriel focused with difficulty to situate herself in what seemed strange surroundings. It slowly came back to her as she looked down the stairs toward a front door that she was alone in the abandoned lighthouse. The bloody handkerchief cued a recollection of her mission to retrieve it, and that explained the absence of her friends. Laboriously she rose and brushed herself off, examining what looked like dried blood on her hand, but with no apparent wound as its source.

Resolved to exit and rejoin her friends, she turned to descend the stairs—to find them occupied by a man, in naval uniform, climbing up toward her. Her heart started at first with surprise and a little alarm, but he seemed to look right through her, past her.

"Sir?" she ventured.

No response—not even any eye movement toward her.

"Excuse me, sir? I've come to retrieve my handkerchief."

The man headed straight toward her, and her alarm grew into a real fear. She knew the house was off limits to the public, but a caretaker should be more civil than to simply menace an apparent intruder, especially someone young, female, and of a decent appearance.

As he neared perilously close, her fleeting perceptions of him gelled into more precise apprehension. The man was middle-aged and extremely ashen of face. He stood a few inches taller than herself, and he wore a blank expression, especially in his eyes, that could almost be seen as threatening. In the span of a second she feared for her own safety, flashing on the shanghai-ing of her own mother—and she stepped sharply back as the man brushed past her, seemingly without notice. He turned and went toward a front bedroom. What tempered her relief at his passing was the realization that he had not actually brushed *past* her; he had brushed *through* her!

Muriel tripped hastily down the staircase and tried to tug at the front door. If this was where the man had entered, he seemed to have relocked it, as it did not move. Strangely, she did not seem to be able to hold on to the knob; it slipped right through her grasp. Glancing up at the landing, she pivoted into the dining room and rushed toward the back of the house to the kitchen door. It seemed stuck, as it also would not budge, and its knob was as slippery as the one on the front door. Suddenly she knew she was trapped in the abandoned light—in what state of being and in what company she knew not.

9—Muriel

Muriel could think of no course of action other than hiding from the menacing man. With both doors unopenable, she could hope for escape only through a window, and that would require some stealth to make sure she was not accosted. She knew few people came close to the abandoned lighthouse these days, but perhaps she could signal to someone walking on the path by the bay. For now she would hide, wait, and try to reason it out.

She ducked from the kitchen into the small back room that served as a study. This seemed as far away from the naval gentleman as she could get in this house. She crouched down in the front corner of the room near a roll-top desk. If he did wander in here, perhaps he wouldn't notice her.

The house was deathly quiet. Muriel was grateful for this. It meant she could keep a clear mind and strain her ears for any sound that might indicate a threat to her safety. She tried to retrace the events just prior to what must have been her blackout. What perplexed her most was the absence of any kind of cut or wound on her hand. She examined it closely now. She thought she recalled trying to slip the bolt on the iron door, and then an accident. The dried blood still present on her hand seemed to verify this memory.

A brief chill caused her to shudder, and she thought she remembered entering a small closet behind the iron door. She recalled through her senses—the icy cold, a low moan, then a falling sensation. Was the fall a dream, or perhaps a hallucination? She was a logical girl, not prone to fits of hysteria. But then how had she ended up back on the floor of the landing?

Muriel furrowed her brow with the effort of concentration. Then she detected a small movement from the corner of her eye. She shrank against the wall in an attempt to be as small and inconspicuous as she could. And then a lady in long skirts skittered as if on air into the room.

Muriel held her breath. The lady walked toward a sewing basket on a trestle table, seemingly intent on some solitary task. Although her very skirts whisked near Muriel on the floor, the lady seemed not to notice, or maybe not to care.

Tentatively Muriel extended a finger to push the skirt hem away from herself. But the skirt would not move, for Muriel's finger passed right through it! She tried again, with the same result. She could see her own hand, and she could see the lady's skirt, both plain as daylight—but both apparently as insubstantial. Both continued to exist visually but to merge into and over each other without any material effect.

The lady floated out of the room, and Muriel was safe—but left in a mental tizzy. It slowly dawned on her that somehow she was existing in another plane. As she tried to add up the clues, she thought they led to a single conclusion. Blood but no wound, no hunger or thirst, spectral companions in this dwelling, insubstantial boundaries of her very own body. She tried a small test by attempting to grab onto the desk leg next to her. Her hand grasped only air—yet the desk leg remained fully visible and there.

Muriel stood and tiptoed over to the study door, a substantial piece of wood standing wide open. She thought to try to close it. Again, her hand would not grasp onto the knob so plainly there. It was like trying to catch a cloud. She moved to the back of the door and shoved at it with her shoulder and the entire weight of her body—but it did not budge, and she found herself standing in front of the door on the threshold. Her body had passed directly through this massive piece of wood!

Peering into the hall and finding it clear, Muriel turned left out of the doorway, walking along the side of the stairs toward the front door, which remained a boundary she could not broach. She climbed the stairs, returning to the place she had awoken from her swoon. Her bloody handkerchief still lay outside the iron door, and she sat down on the floor near it.

Her mind was pulling blanks, and Muriel was frightened. She had tried every logical means of escape that occurred to her—and her companions in this house unsettled her. Who *were* they? And now, who was she?

A rattling noise rose up the staircase from the front door, and Muriel's heart started. She stood, descended the turn in the stairs, and saw the door quickly swing open. Harold stood in the doorway, his silhouette outlined like a shadow against the waning light behind him.

He paused there, accustoming his eyes to the dimmer light within the house walls, and then he said her name!

"Muriel?" he called out softly, and then louder, "Muriel, are you in here?"

"Yes, yes, oh here I am!" she responded with a sense of relief and delight. Laughing, she stepped forward so he might see her clearly, here at the turn of the second set of stairs.

"Mur-i-el!" he called out even louder, stepping into the small foyer.

"Yes! Here!" she said again, but he only glanced around him and then began to climb the stairs.

"Oh, Harold," Muriel exclaimed, "I'm so glad you came back for me."

Harold's head lifted toward her, but again he did not respond, and his face remained expressionless. She moved another pace forward so that she stood at the top of the bottom step. He surely could not miss her there. But Harold reached the main stair top and ignored her entirely, instead quickly bending down to pick up the bloody handkerchief.

She stood next to him as he examined the handkerchief and frowned. He began to look all around the hallway, and again he called her name.

"Muriel!" He sounded alarmed.

She put out her hand to touch his shoulder, only inches away from where she stood. As with the desk leg and the study door, her hand was clearly visible yet passed through him without effect. Her heart sank at this, but, strangely, she thought he responded to what she could only call her non-touch. He lifted his eyes in her direction with a puzzled expression.

Still clutching her handkerchief, he turned toward the back bedroom, then returned to the hall and checked each of the other upper rooms. Muriel followed him in his quest. When he came back to the top of the stairs, he climbed the spiral set with Muriel as his shadow and focused on the iron door, trying its catch and rattling it back and forth. Nothing budged.

He stuck his head into the light tower itself, and then she had to scurry out of his way as he descended to the landing again.

But then, *I suppose he might have stepped right through me*, she thought, realizing her own insubstantial invisibility. And with that she had fully understood her helplessness.

10—Muriel

All those events were so long ago, and Muriel seldom even revisited them in her memory. It was too troubling to realize that her friends were dead and gone by now, the manly Harold somewhere a ghost like herself. She had long since come to terms with her apparent invisibility. Mostly the material world did not interact with what she still thought of as her body, even though her conscious self was strong and active. And of course, she'd discovered that with an act of intense focus she could force the living to notice and pay attention. But why bother? What was to be gained for her?

In the same vein, her mind was slowly admitting that her father was gone from this earth as well. Her nightly mission of sending out her feeble signal light was a futile and doomed effort. Its only purpose was to give a structure to her aimless being in shapeless time. She no longer ate or drank. She could only meander through the lighthouse rooms, trying to avoid the others—whom she now knew were ghosts like herself.

With her longing for connectedness, she thought it a pity that somehow all the lost souls at loose in this house could not unite into some kind of community. At least it would be a comfort to hear others' stories and to learn how they had coped with their change to this other state of—she wanted to call it "existence." She wondered if the naval gentleman had died while on the job. She wondered what kind of family the long-skirted woman had and what kind of task she was so intent on performing.

But these lost souls seemed truly lost to anything but some kind of personal mission. Perhaps they had not discovered that, like her, they might exercise their will to break out of their solitude, at least temporarily. They floated about in the house oblivious to each other, and they all wore blank stares that seemed to be looking out beyond this world. Muriel wondered what had determined the moment of their fixed attention. What did they seek? Like her, did they hope for rescue or escape?

If she were to be realistic and abandon hope of her father's return, Muriel needed to reassess her own options. What end could she envision to this intolerable imprisonment? *I am dead,* she thought, *but not gone.* And that was the sticking point. She had disappeared down the closet-hole, and no one had known precisely of her demise. Her life was waiting for closure, the end beyond death.

And her wait had already been too long. What she had begun to imagine now was discovery of her bones and removal of them to a proper grave. Perhaps it was too much to hope for a stone marker or mourners who might visit that gravesite and remember her with a tribute of posies. But at least that marked grave would mean that her short life had mattered to someone, anyone. Even a random visitor who wandered among the markers could see her name and perhaps wonder how her life was cut off with her only in her teenage years.

In the midst of this aimless musing, her eye caught the movement of a man and a girl walking up the steps toward the lighthouse. Muriel remembered her experiment in focusing her will on another passer-by, and on a whim she tried to signal to this pair, who brought to mind herself and her own father, oh so long ago. The girl seemed about her own age, and Muriel's heart ached with longing to be with family once again.

Although she could make no sound she knew they might hear, Muriel waved her hand toward the window in a vigorous motion, at the same time focusing her will on them to look up and take notice. As she signaled, she cried out, "Help me! Help me! Help me!"

And then a miracle: the man looked directly toward her. He stopped, said something to his daughter, and then raised his arm, pointing toward the upper window of the lighthouse! She waved even more frantically—and then she felt weak, depleted of will. The man and his daughter resumed walking. She noticed that they continued to climb the steps to her house, but she had only enough energy to return to her perpetual nest, protected just inside that fateful but now camouflaged iron door.

11—Amelia

She hoped no one driving by on the bridge had recognized her. This green get-up of Dad's devising probably disguised any of her distinctive features, thank goodness. For here she was, acting like a nerdly daughter of a nerd father, tromping through the coastal rain singing a silly song at the top of her lungs. Seeing the pirate ship slip beneath them, though, was the thrill of a lifetime, she must admit. Standing at the top of the bridge's rise surrounded by mist, and then the full sails emerging, white from white in the fog, the silence of its movement unsettling—this was otherworldly to her. She felt transported into a past where she was living a different life, still herself but with new aspects to her character.

Lately she had felt some twinges of what she could only term adulthood. The loss of her mother had been a shock she was unprepared to put into any kind of rhyme or reason. Why would a loving and beautiful spirit be put through the suffering of a horrible cancer? And what kind of God would leave a needy teen-age girl abandoned without a mother, and a vulnerable father to try to make his own way through a daily life his mind was too distracted to handle?

She and Dad had limped along since Mom's death, clinging strongly to each other. But try as he might, he simply could not understand her teen-ager's world or empathize with her emotional ups and downs. She knew that her fluctuating moods confused and frustrated him. She worked hard to mask her acute intelligence at school so that she could stay "in" with the popular crowd. Belonging was important to her. She needed society outside of her shrinking family unit if she was to have any kind of future.

Yet she also had an inkling of Pah-rent's deep hurt. It had created a canyon of emptiness and loss in him that she felt inadequate to fill, yet she felt obligated to try. She needed to be there for him now. He really had no one else. She tried to bring forward qualities she felt she'd inherited from her mother, and she could see this delighted him. Perhaps the mirror, or ghost, of her mother within herself was the way Mom could remain with them, living on within her daughter.

So it was obligation to others rather than personal desires that dominated her actions more and more lately. Her mind would flit to images of her friends and idle times trying on outfits and practicing dance moves, but then Dad's faraway look would bring her to the here and now—and trying to keep him tied to this world, whatever unexpected troubles life might bring them.

She swallowed hard, pushing these thoughts to the back of her mind, and beamed up at Dad through dewy eyelashes as they descended from the rise at the mid-point of the bridge. Right now he seemed content, even happy. The lighthouse was in clear view and seemed close, but then as they neared the north end of the bridge it became obscured by the trees. Just a turn left and a short walk up a slight hill, and they'd be at the foot of its staircase.

"Can you imagine what it would have been like, living here at the lighthouse even before the bridge was built?" Dad ventured. "The harbor would not have seen constant traffic of the grand tall ships, but there was ferry service back and forth, and a stream of fishing boats to be sure. No instant communication in those days, and it took a lot longer to move from place to place. We've almost lost the sense of the river as a roadway, but so it was—and even the beach itself. The wagon carrying the mail would race along the surf at low tide as part of its regular route."

"So do you think your great grandfather might have walked along right where we are now?" she asked.

"He certainly could have, Amelia. Both here, where the river widens, and just upriver past the bridge there where you can see the boat moorings. He would have kept a keen eye and a sharp ear alert to the rise and fall of the tides. Getting out to sea and back safely was more of a challenge before the building of the jetties. See how they reach out like two long arms to shelter this point where fresh and salt water meet?"

"How sad that nobody lives in the lighthouse anymore," she replied. "That would have kept our history more alive." The house and its tower had popped back into view as they walked up the hill.

"The big lighthouse on the Head serves a better purpose," Dad replied, "as it's able to send out a beam to ships at sea and orient them, keeping them from running too close to the rocky shore. This small light was a beacon only to the harbor itself. Tomorrow if it's clear we can walk out on the south jetty, and you can see how close that other lighthouse seems, just to the north but higher and further out on the point."

"Gee, Dad, walking gives you a whole different view of how the land fits together. . . . You know that story I read last night?"

"Oh, you mean that old legend about—what was her name?—Muriel, the orphan?"

"NOT an orphan, Dad! She and her dad were searching the sea for her shanghaied mother!"

"Where'd you pick up that word, shanghaied?" he commented.

"It was in the story! Doesn't it mean kidnapped?"

"Well, yes—just in an old-fashioned way."

"So anyway, this story says she's still trapped in the house, and nobody knows if she died in there or *what* happened."

The house had temporarily disappeared behind the trees, but as they turned to climb the twenty-one steps to the winding walkway up to the door, it sprang back into view. Suddenly Dad stopped in his tracks and grabbed her arm.

"Omigod, Amelia!" he said in a strange, high voice. Her body jumped in surprise.

"WHAT? What is it? What's wrong?"

"I thought I saw a face in the upper window! Someone is waving frantically! Oh, her face is so pale, and sad! See, there, up there?" He placed his head next to hers and extended his arm along a common sight-line.

She gazed beyond his arm eagerly—and saw only the placid lighthouse with its large, square windows like blank eyes watching the harbor. Her own eyes scanned the face of her father—could this be an uncharacteristic joke on his part? Was he teasing her? She found no clue in his look.

"Da-ad," she said, just in case.

12—Hal

Amelia was hardly ever this carefree around adults, especially her serious scientist father, as he knew she thought of him. Hal took advantage of the moment as they came off the bridge and approached the lighthouse to build on his daughter's unusual interest in this myth of the disappearance of Muriel. As they turned up the steps leading to the house, he pretended to see a ghostly face in the upper window and milked the dramatic moment. Amelia seemed completely taken in.

He wasn't entirely amused by his own prank, however, for the heck of it was he thought he *had* seen a face, just quickly flitting by. Of course with the mist and the shadows and all, how could he be sure? And maybe his imagination was working overtime these days, as they had been forced to look Death directly in the face.

Losing someone who was integral to your daily life was a horrible jolt that opened up inevitable philosophical speculations about the nature of existence. What was it that made a person that particular familiar being that you knew and loved? A personality, a spirit, a presence—all unique and recognizable—yet it is here in one moment, warmly alive, palpable, and in an instant gone from us forever—in that form. Maybe "forever" was too final a word. Or at least Hal wanted to believe so. The scientist in him understood biological vitality— a beating heart, circulation of fluids, inhalation and exhalation that kept our spirit within the confines of a material body. But what happened to that spirit when the body could hold it no longer? Did it dissipate into nothingness?

How cruel a joke that would be by anyone's god, he thought. What were the alternatives? Did the spirit keep its print of individual personality and remain, but invisible to our sensory world? Could places retain the spiritual imprint of actual people who had walked there, breathed there, filled that space?

In moments of distress he thought he could feel Gillian's hand still smoothing his brow or her gentle voice calming him. Was her "self" imprinted onto the synapses of his brain? If that were the case, then she did live on but within him. He carried and nurtured her spirit within his own memory—and could experience her still through memory as a sensory reality.

He snapped to full attention as he and his daughter neared the door to the house and its squat tower, which had contained the old beacon light.

They opened the large wooden door and were instantly transported back into the nineteenth century. You simply didn't see houses built on this model anymore, with such separation of spaces defining daily activities. A well-walled room was devised, he knew, partly to help contain the heat for its occupants. They regarded the floor plan laid out on an easel in the small foyer. The design was boxy and simple—a room at each corner, clearly defined for cooking, dining, sitting, or studying—with a solid staircase anchoring the center of the house and rising just before them. Another set of stairs, circular in shape, was visible just beyond the top of the landing.

He saw his daughter look to the top of the stairs and then immediately begin climbing up.

"Amelia, don't you want to see the down-stairs first?" he called out to her.

She paused and turned her face toward him. Her eyes were wide, and he read in them a combination of wonder and trepidation.

"I know it was right up here that Muriel disappeared," she said in a hushed tone. "I have to look at the spot, Dad. It's like she's pulling me to her."

She turned and continued her progress up the staircase.

Not sure if his daughter was fooling with him all in the spirit of his prank on her, Hal moved quickly up the lower steps and shadowed Amelia to the landing.

"It's sort of spooky," she announced. "Can you feel it, Dad? A chill right here at the bottom of the spiral stairs? And something smells kind of funny."

Amelia raised her eyes toward him again, this time filled with awe and wonder.

"Since when does my worldly daughter believe in ghosts from the days of yore?" he asked, trying to shrug off his own feeling of eeriness here at the gateway to the iron door.

They made their way up the second staircase. At the top she lifted her hand almost as if it levitated of its own accord, and it came to rest, fingers extended, on the wall where once hung the strange metal door. How would she have known its location? She seemed to have been pulled to that spot by instinct.

"The wall is cold," she proclaimed, then fell silent, and she froze in that position as if communicating with another world.

The small hairs on the back of Hal's neck stood as if in anticipation—or fear.

13—Amelia

She was grateful that Pah-rent had caught up with her at the top of the stairs. From the moment they had stepped over the threshold into the lighthouse, Amelia had felt an urge like the pull of a magnetic force to this very spot near the top of the spiral set. Standing here in front of the blank wall was eerie, though, like nothing she'd ever felt before. She wasn't sure what "uncanny" meant, but that's the word that popped into her mind. She had no idea at all what would come next.

She had the feeling that something was expected of her, some action she needed to perform. Until now, she'd never had to act on her own, and she liked knowing that her dad was at her side. With his support, she knew she was ready—ready to become more like her strong mother, ready to let her own character blossom into its full potential. Being without her friends was forcing her to be more self-reliant.

The chill she felt at first near the place of the iron door was gone now, and she removed her hand from the wall's surface.

A tour guide was coming up the stairs, and as he looked up toward them he called out, "Do you feel a coolness there by the wall? It's perfectly normal. We've got that and the top of the spiral stairs blocked off for visitors' safety. There was an iron door that opened into a cupboard, and below it dropped straight down to the elements. They must have used the opening with a pulley system to bring heavier items directly up to the second story. Wouldn't want a lovely young lady like yourself to slip through and be lost to us!"

He smiled. They moved down the spiral stairs to join him on the first landing.

"Now you can walk into the front bedrooms here and get a pretty good view across the bay and toward the open water. But you can understand from that vantage point why they needed a light in a better spot. This one just has limited visibility out at sea."

"Thanks for the information," Pah-rent said to the man. "We'll do just that," he added and took a couple of steps down the hall toward the front of the house.

"Um," Amelia broached without following him.

"Do you have a question?" the guide asked.

Pah-rent turned and looked back at them both.

"Um, does the lighthouse have any ghosts?"

"Oh, that old myth," the guide said with a chuckle. "Don't you worry, little lady! The screaming meanies only haunt this place after dark."

"Surely you're joking," Pah-rent chimed in.

"Of course, of course. Don't want to scare your daughter here. Everybody wants the old lighthouse to be haunted. . . . Well, every once in a while we get reports of lights floating around in the tower, but it's just folks' active imaginations, I'm afraid. You're safe as can be—nothing at all to fear."

"I'm *not* afraid," Amelia replied.

"Good for you—a heroic gal you are," he said, and turned to descend the stairs.

"But what about Muriel?" Amelia called out. The guide froze in mid-step.

"How do you know that name?" he asked without moving.

And then he turned to face her.

"How do *you* know that name?" she returned boldly.

"It's just that . . . not too many people are familiar with the real story," he rushed to fill in.

"So the story is real? I just knew it!" she said.

"Lots of folks have heard old wives' tales," he continued. "I can't think of a single light-house from here to Mexico that doesn't have some kind of popular lore attached to it—kind of like historical sites in England, or Scotland, or anywhere there's a long history. People tell of seeing mysterious floating lights at night or headless figures wandering, always searching for something."

"Have *you* seen her?" Amelia looked directly into the guide's eyes.

"Imagination can play tricks on anybody, especially by the light of the setting sun," the guide back-pedaled. "But this is the twenty-first century, and I assure you this is not a spook-house. You can learn about our history here, but we'll leave the ghosts to Ripley's Believe-it-or-Not down on the bayfront."

As the guide delivered this pronouncement, Amelia felt the temperature around her dropping quickly. The chill enveloped her, like icy fingers reaching out from the place of the iron door. She smiled at the guide—and shivered.

14—MURIEL

Her energy was slowly returning. It had been given a jolt by the success of her experiment. Muriel had extended her focused will to the man and his daughter near the bay, and this will had reached them. Like a beacon it had brought them into the lighthouse, and now they stood just beyond the door of her refuge. She wondered, if they were a link to the present world, might they be able to help her escape from this prison—and be laid at last to rest? And was she ready to give up this limbo for an even greater unknown?

She rose, smoothed her skirt, and stepped through the iron door and its camouflaging wall onto the upper landing, then slipped soundlessly down to the main hallway, where she found company. Muriel stood shoulder to shoulder with Amelia. It was uncanny how much, even across all these decades, the two teen-age girls resembled each other. Muriel could inspect her modern counterpart at leisure. She admired the gentle curls of her shoulder-length hair and the confidence of Amelia's clear gaze. She took special note of Amelia's clothing, which seemed odd but sensible—fashioned for comfort and ease of movement. It was still modest, Muriel thought, but stretchy, and it wouldn't bog you down as her skirts tended to do.

As Muriel continued her inspection, Amelia hugged herself.

"Dad, suddenly it's so cold! Do you feel it?" she asked.

The man, who was standing nearby, reached out his hand toward his daughter. Muriel stepped quickly to one side to avoid his reach, and he frowned.

"What is it, Dad?" the girl responded.

He paused, and then said, "Well, as I put out my hand I felt a blast of chilly air pass over me. It's odd, as there seem to be no drafts in this solid house. Let's check the view from the front windows and then we can finish up downstairs."

The father and daughter turned to walk down the hall toward the south-facing bedrooms. Muriel floated along at their heels. If she could steel her resolve to try to make contact, she'd need to find the right opportunity. Maybe this pair, so like Muriel and her own father, would be the means of her release—if she was ready for that next step on her journey. Maybe time was less a line than a circle. Maybe patterns repeated themselves, and maybe the patterns could intersect and influence each other.

Something in the obvious affection of the pair reminded her of times spent fondly with her own father. He had always been protective of her, and after her mother had been lost, he stepped in to be both father and mother to Muriel. The way this father leaned toward his daughter to point out something in the view made Muriel think of the times on the ship when her own father had first taught her and then supervised her attempts at fishing. She'd held the rod while he stood nearby, net in hand.

"Now first cast it out, and then your line and bobber will drag along as the ship sails. The fish will spot your bait moving in the wake and will take it as live prey. When the big one bites you'll feel a strong pull, and you must tug back as hard as you can. Reel in when the fish seems to rest, then let it play when it pulls out again. I'm here to help if you need me. If you can yank it up, I can reach out and net it. Or if you can swing it onto the deck, we'll conk it on the head, and there's your supper, fresh from the bounty of our sea."

There were more tender moments that now began to crowd her memory. After the shanghai incident in San Francisco, they'd hit the seas hard hoping to track the ship carrying her mother away. But the seas hit Muriel hard too, and she spent much of her time below deck feeling queasy.

On the occasions when she could no longer hold down her lunch, her father always hovered nearby, wiping her brow with a cool cloth, saying "There, there, my little one. Think calming thoughts now. Keep your eyes steady on one object, and plant your feet firmly on the boards. Soon enough the rises and falls should feel like second nature to you."

But she had never developed her sea-legs, and her father thought it best to give her a respite from the chase. He had gently deposited her here in Newport, making sure she would be safe and well-tended to. Before he returned to the sea and his quest, the two of them had walked on the beach together and on the same path along the bay that had brought this father and daughter to her, the pair that now stood before her regarding the view.

It was now or perhaps never, she thought. As the pair stood at the front hall window, Muriel focused as hard as she could to make her presence known. If they believed in her existence, that would be the first step toward communication and then maybe their help in finding her release. If anyone might sense her and then listen to her, she felt in her soul it would be this girl so like herself.

The father and daughter peered out the window, pointing at possible whale spouts in the distance—or perhaps the bobbing heads of harbor seals closer in. Muriel closed her eyes and concentrated all her will on Amelia, trying to make a connection.

"Help me," she thought over and over. "I stand directly behind you."

Suddenly a small cry escaped from Amelia's mouth.

The father placed his arm protectively around her and said, "Honey, what's wrong?"

Amelia glanced behind her with fear in her eyes.

"Dad, I saw that girl's face reflected in the window! She's here in the house, and she's standing right behind us!"

15–Hal

In the days that followed their lighthouse excursion, Hal and Amelia would puzzle over the chain of events that had led to an apparent sighting of a ghost. And not just "a ghost," but one with a specific place and a specific past, according to the story.

Amelia had been agitated by the reflection she saw in the window. Hal had hurried her out of the lighthouse without even wandering through the first floor. The flow of adrenaline spurred them on at a quick pace, down the stairs leading to the house, up the hill to the bridge, and across the bridge in a blur of speed back to their condo with the tower on the south side of the river's bay.

Their quickly-beating hearts and their swift pace kept them from any discussion of the events. Both father and daughter were lost in private thought, each pondering the logic and reality of this outing's experience: first, the disorienting mist, then the magic of the pirate ship, followed by the eeriness of Hal's vision of a face at the lighthouse window.

Add to these their sense of another presence inside, the inexplicable chill in front of "Muriel's door," and it was difficult to explain away Amelia's experience of Muriel herself palpably present behind them on the landing.

Back in the condo Hal helped Amelia remove her soggy rain gear in silence. They shook out their ponchos in the entry and tugged off their boots, now sodden with rain.

Padding into the small kitchen in stocking feet, Hal said, "Honey, let's have a cup of hot chocolate to bring us back to life. What do you say?"

"Sounds good," his daughter managed to croak out. "Dad, I'm super-chilled, inside and out." She was shaking.

Hal finished pouring milk into a saucepan and placing it on the burner. He bustled over to the cast iron stove and broke some kindling into sticks he could easily light, then placed a Presto-log in the middle of the tongues of flame. Amelia plunked down at the spool of rigging pretending to be a dining table, and Hal reached over to rub her neck and shoulders.

"Here, let's get your blood flowing again," he said as he massaged vigorously. "Unfair of me to make you venture out in the elements on such an inclement day. Look at this, even your hair is damp. No wonder you're cold."

He grabbed a small towel from the kitchen counter and dabbed it at the scraggly tendrils around her face and nape.

Amelia bowed her head to help with this process, and then she froze. Hal paused in his toweling, and both of them riveted their gaze on the book that still lay on the table from breakfast: *The Haunted Light at Newport by the Sea.* It was like the elephant in the room. Neither one of them wanted to mention it, but it loomed before them, unavoidable.

Hal laid down his towel and tended to the now-warm milk, adding sugar and cocoa and pouring the mixture into mugs. He returned to the table with their hot drinks and sat down by his daughter. Both of them sipped eagerly.

"Mmm, feels good going down," Amelia commented, then looked imploringly at her father.

"Are you warming up a bit now?" he asked. "That fire's sending some heat our way." They sat in a silence that became more and more unbearable. The fire crackled, and the rain lashed at the windows. They sipped their cocoa.

"Dad," Amelia finally began. "I know what I saw. And you saw her too from below, but you tried to make a joke out of it."

"Honey, there is no such thing as ghosts. Listen to your father, the scientist. Sure, we have feelings, and memories, of those who have gone on, but visualizing them is just the product of an over-active imagination. They no longer walk the earth, as much as we'd like to keep them here with us."

The face of his own wife appeared in his mind as he spoke these words, and he felt the pang of his own loss.

Amelia took a long pause before responding. She cupped her hands around her cocoa mug, staring down at the table. Her eyes could not avoid the book of the ghost sitting there so prominently. Her face wore a distracted frown.

Finally she spoke, enunciating each word with an unaccustomed deliberateness.

"I read about her, and I felt her presence, and then I saw her face. Are you telling me I imagined her exact facial features? Here, I can sketch her for you if you don't believe me."

Amelia reached down into her backpack lying against the wall and pulled out her drawing tablet. She began penciling in strong lines without hesitation, and a girl's face began to materialize. The girl's hair was in an old-fashioned style, pulled up in braids behind her ears, and she gazed toward the viewer with a sense of hope and expectancy.

From across the table Hal watched this face come slowly alive. Amelia made one last shading under the cheekbones with her pencil and then turned the tablet toward Hal for his inspection.

Against all his better reason, he felt goosebumps forming on his arms—for he recognized, without a doubt, the face of the girl who had gestured to him from the lighthouse window.

16—AMELIA

The face of the ghost girl was firmly etched in Amelia's mind, and she'd had no trouble in reproducing it on her sketchpad to show Pah-rent. He seemed to want to explain it all away, but in retrospect she viewed that entire day as a mystical turning point in her life.

There really was no other conclusion if you added up the clues. First she'd found the old book with Muriel's story, as if it had been waiting for her at the bottom of the chest for who knows how many years. This was followed by the magical appearance of the pirate ship straight out of Muriel's story and her own time. Amelia now read that as an omen, foretelling her own meeting with Muriel. Dad had seen Muriel in the window, though he didn't want to admit it, and Amelia had felt a magnetic pull to the spot where Muriel had been lost in the lighthouse, as if the hand of destiny had guided her there. In a sense the appearance of Muriel's face behind her in the window was no surprise, but rather a natural progression of the events of the day.

Amelia knew she had been chosen. She simply needed to figure out a plan of action. Although Amelia had heard no voice, she sensed the ghost girl was in trouble and needed help. The beacon lights and her face in the window were messages enough.

Early next morning she decided to conduct some research on her own. If the ghost was relying on Amelia as she sensed, she'd need to make a plan. She could smell the strong coffee Pah-rent had brewed as she made her way to the kitchen. The table had been cleared off to make room for the breakfast dishes.

"Juice, honey?" Dad asked as she plunked down in her chair. "Hey, you haven't caught a cold, have you?" he continued.

"Dad, what happened to that book?"

"Your sketchbook? I put it down by your backpack."

"No-o-o, the book about Muriel that was sitting right here. I want to read it again for clues."

"Clues about what, sweetheart? We had an emotional and imaginative day yesterday, didn't we? Let's put it behind us and keep it as an amusing memory. Years from now we'll marvel at the vision of the pirate ship and laugh at my silly joke about a ghostly face in the lighthouse window."

Amelia frowned, then looked Pah-rent directly in the eye.

"I can't do that. Somehow the ghost girl has reached out to me, and I must help her. I just need to figure out how."

At a loss for words, he sipped at his coffee and examined the face of his daughter closely. Finally he spoke quietly.

"Just now you reminded me so much of your mother. . . . How do you intend to proceed?" he asked, and Amelia let out a sigh of relief.

This meant Pah-rent was on her side, for once, and that he would squelch his habit of scientific analysis in favor of Amelia's own intuition.

"I'm going to take the book and read her story carefully again," Amelia said. "And then maybe we can get to know old Newport better. Maybe if we follow some of her footsteps I can understand her times, and her experience. And maybe seeing the world through her eyes will lead me to the right course of action to release her. But, Dad," and Amelia raised a clear and open gaze to meet that of her father, "I'm going to need your help, if you're willing."

Amelia could not have foreseen that this strategy lent a magic to her mission. The father and daughter, both plunged for months into a kind of aimless grief, would now make an alliance that would shape their summer vacation into a quest. Amelia would lead the way, with Pah-rent standing right behind her as support. His agreement to be her partner was a vote of confidence in her own judgment and her way of viewing the world. And suddenly Amelia felt very grown up, and she sat up a little straighter in her chair.

Sensing their new alliance, Amelia decided to broach the taboo subject. Instead of avoiding the death they were still confronting every day, she'd been hoping she could share her grief.

"You said just now I reminded you of Mom. . . . Dad, I sure do miss her, and I don't know how to keep my memories of her. So much of her love she showed us in little gestures that I hardly noticed, how she'd lay out my school things right by the door, or how she'd put funny notes in with my lunch. It used to embarrass me, but now I'd do anything to have those back. And I feel like she's fading even more, the longer she's been gone."

Dad gave her a tender look, and he came over quickly to hug her hard. But he said nothing, and she began to sob gently.

"How do you go on without her?" Amelia squeezed out between gasps. Swallowing deliberately to regain composure, she said, "You just seem so calm and rational every day. You move ahead as if life is just the same whether she's here or not. And sometimes I just can't stand it that's she's gone." She lifted her tear-stained face to look at him.

"Oh, honey." He hugged her even harder. "I'm hurting too," he said at last. "You are the last remaining good thing of my life, and I'm clinging to you for all I'm worth."

"Dad? . . . Do you think Mom's turned into a ghost somewhere?"

"Oh, my, what a question. I think this Muriel business might be upsetting you." He dabbed at her tears with a tissue.

"Sometimes I think I hear her talking to me, and then I think it must just be in my own head. Have you seen her, Dad? Or has she spoken to you?"

"Amelia. My treasure. Yes, I can see your mother's face in my mind's eye. And I can remember her laughter and her voice almost as if she were speaking here and now. What we have to understand is that our memories of her keep her real for us. It's a good thing. A good thing that she talks to you in your mind. A good thing that you remember her loving gestures and that her caring actions toward you have outlived her time on earth. You are now, and you always will be, a result of your mother and her love." He tapped her lightly on the chest. "And you must feel the warmth of that love in your heart and know that it was and still is real. She will never totally leave us. We are not abandoned." He tried a smile.

"I've felt I have to fill in the gaps she left behind for you," Amelia responded softly.

"That's a big responsibility for a little girl. You help me every day by just being you. You and I, we're the family team now. . . . And I think we should find out more about what's up with that lighthouse, don't you?"

Pah-rent rose and, without another word, stepped over to the refrigerator. He reached up and rummaged around in the high cupboard above it and pulled down the "Muriel book," handing it directly to his daughter.

"Just let me know when you're ready—and tell me what to do," he said. "We're off on our adventure, and you have the lead."

17—Hal

His daughter took the "Muriel book" and retreated to her bedroom. He didn't know what kind of "clues" she thought she might find there, but it was clear to him the idea of an entrapped, motherless ghost girl had struck a chord in her. While he didn't want to encourage frivolous ideas or behavior, he had spontaneously decided to give Amelia free reign in her Muriel research. This might be a project that would bring father and daughter closer together as they worked through their grief.

As he tidied up the kitchen he let his mind wander. He was emotionally exhausted after that conversation about death with Amelia. Since losing Gillian he'd developed a daily habit of making a spiritual check-up of everyone important to him. One by one he brought them to mind. The living, he wondered about the course of their day, the details of what they were doing. The departed, he rehearsed some kind of personal memory so that they lived on in a way, recollecting a pleasant memory or something they did together. They were still part of his experience, part of his personal universe of what mattered.

He worked his way through his tally of loved ones and got to his daughter. He viewed this moment as transitional for her, and it thrust him into his own quandary. His entire life he'd devoted himself to developing an ability for rational thinking based on verifiable data. This made him wary of jumping to conclusions, and he always looked for simple concrete reasons to what might appear as mysterious. Science itself was a kind of magic at times. Repeated patterns were everywhere, and they were often invisible to the untrained eye. He knew this habit sometimes made him seem unfeeling or detached in others' perception of him.

In his nuclear family Gillian had been the one to make an owie better or soothe Amelia after a nightmare. Hal had been there for them as an anchor, but he was busy with work, and even when he was home his mind often remained focused on a work project.

If his exterior made him seem distant, it was far different from the condition of his heart and spirit. The women in his life kept him vibrant and alive. He had learned to swallow back emotion when it surged through him, and he presented a logical, analytical face to the world.

It was not an overstatement to say that their recent experiences in the lighthouse had unsettled his trust in rationality. He knew the difference between an imagined event and a real one, and he had indeed seen a girl gesturing to them from the upstairs window. After feeling that grave-like chill at the top of the stairs and hearing his own daughter's description of a face of someone invisible standing behind them but reflected in the window, Hal was just about ready to become a believer. Maybe this ghost, poor young Muriel, did exist—if that was the right word. Maybe some kind of energy willed from a consciousness could materialize into a temporary vision.

And if he could accept that premise, then what was to be done about her haunting of them? Why had Muriel chosen them—and Amelia in particular—and what was her message? Others before them had seen evidence of the ghost, but she had not reached out to them. Her spiritual energy seemed to be accomplishing two things of which Hal would normally be skeptical. She wandered as a specter, apparently trapped, within the walls of the lighthouse. And this spiritual manifestation of someone who *had* lived, more than a hundred years ago, was somehow violating time, or our understanding of how time worked. Her personality seemed still to be individual and separate, and it wanted to communicate from the past to initiate some kind of action in the present. His present. His daughter's present.

Again he asked himself, what did she want of them? He passed his mind over the details of the story Amelia had recounted to him from the small book, details of a girl who was a victim of circumstances that had torn her family apart and left her stranded. Whatever had happened to end her life so abruptly in the lighthouse had taken her in essence as an orphan. Now her soul was still bereft of family, and she was searching for completion. And the realization came to Hal in a flash: Muriel wanted some kind of ending. She wanted rest, and peace. The very instant this thought flashed through his mind, Amelia rushed back into the kitchen, waving the small book containing Muriel's story.

"Dad, we have to find the cemetery. Do you know where it is? We have to see if Muriel is there or not."

Hal mentally ticked off the places he knew away from the bay and the coastline here in a Newport he'd visited since he was a child.

"If she's buried, it would be at the Eureka Cemetery up on the hill, honey. Yes, we can go there today if you want."

"I think this is the clue to our mystery, Dad. If we don't find her at the cemetery, we need to get her a spot there. She wants us to help her find . . ."

"Closure," father and daughter said in unison.

18–AMELIA

Pah-rent was backing the car out of the garage, and they were going to drive up the hill to the pioneer cemetery. He had pulled out his laptop long enough for Amelia to look at its web site on-line. The cemetery had been incorporated in 1889, but graves had been gathered there years before that. In all likelihood if Muriel had found a final resting place, it would be in Eureka. The story itself remained silent on what happened after her disappearance. Even if her body was not located, maybe someone had made a memorial for her, some kind of marker in the graveyard. If not, Amelia could completely relate to the restlessness of this spirit. Searching through the cemetery for some trace of her would be a good beginning in figuring out how to help the ghost girl in distress.

Amelia got into the car and they headed toward Highway 101, then Dad navigated onto Rte. 20 going east, away from the bay, the lighthouse, and the sea. Father and daughter remained silent for a while, each lost in private thought.

Finally Amelia spoke.

"You know, Dad, since we've been here I've noticed how the ocean really gets into you."

"How so, honey?"

"Well, first there's that constant noise. Everybody talks about the soothing swoosh of the waves, but it's more like a roar. Kind of like being next to the freeway."

They laughed together at this irony.

"Not exactly restful, is it?" Dad replied.

"And the intense light. You can't get away from it, especially near sunset. I'm glad it's cool, 'cause I've had to wear my shades every time it's not raining."

"All that water creates an enormous reflective surface," Dad began analytically. "I seem to remember from my own childhood that from the cemetery you can still see the great Pacific, though it's more than a mile distant. If you maintain a sense that the ocean is generally to the west, it's a great way to keep yourself oriented. Somehow you always know more or less where you are, by virtue of the placement of the water."

Dad turned left on Harney Street and almost immediately right on 3d Street. Amelia saw a large funeral home straight ahead, and then they were in the deep coastal woods on a curving road seemingly far from civilization. Although it wasn't actively raining today, the foliage still seemed wet, and very lush. Drops glistened on leaves and fronds, becoming multi-colored gems when the sun hit them just right.

"I've been thinking, maybe that's Muriel's problem, Dad."

"What, sweetie?"

"She's disoriented. She doesn't have a place, her place. Her father dropped her here, in a town that wasn't home, and she had to fend for herself. Without you, I don't know how I'd even get along. Wherever you are, or wherever we are together, I guess that's my home."

Hal detected a small catch in his daughter's voice, and he glanced over at her. She was staring straight ahead as a small tear made its way down her cheek. Without a word he reached over and covered her hand with his own.

They saw the Eureka sign and pulled left into the cemetery, which was situated among giant trees. It seemed peaceful, untouched by time. Dad parked near the little caretaker's house, and Amelia found a tissue and blew her nose.

"Ah, yes, just as I remember it," Dad commented as they got out of the car.

Sure enough, the ocean glinted there out to the horizon. It looked like the edge of the world from up here on the hill.

"What a great view these Newporters have! And where would you like to begin, Ms. Detective?"

There was a general map of the cemetery tacked to the door of the shed, and Amelia located the area marked as "original." It held the oldest graves. Situating herself by checking the location of the sea against the map, she pointed.

"Over here, Dad. This is the section with the ones from Muriel's time."

They crossed the drive and began wandering along the gentle slope in an absolute absence of the sounds of civilization. The massive trees were impressive, probably older than some of the graves' inhabitants, and their leaf cover mottled the ground with patterns of darkness and light. Some of the grave markers stood upright—or nearly so—and on these the inscriptions had been almost worn away. Here and there you could make out a date, 1869 and the like, so Amelia knew they were in the right area.

She couldn't understand her friends' fear of graveyards. Too many zombie movies, maybe. This place was timeless and magical, filled with the natural sounds of buzzing life. Rather than fear, she felt a sort of reverence for the human stories buried here, and she wondered about the details of this life or that one. She paused at grave after grave, her imagination leaping into the possibilities of each person's story.

"Amelia, take a look at this," Pah-rent called out to her. He was standing in front of an amazing tree, unlike any she'd ever seen.

"I'll bet the natives called that the tree-of-many-trunks," she responded.

The tree covered a broad area with its foliage, that rose from several trunks fanning out from the main column.

"Aren't you the historian," Dad said. "What exactly are you hoping to find here? What should I be looking for?"

She had joined him near the tree, and they were standing by the sequence of graves, at least three generations, of the Nye family—the original John Nye of the nineteenth century for whom Nye Beach was named, and his children and grandchildren, all in a row. This cemetery was a treasure trove of history.

"I wanna find Muriel's grave," Amelia responded. "I can't read the names on some of these stones. I hoped someone, somebody who knew her, would at least make a memorial to her, and then we could check to see if there was an actual burial, see if she'd been laid to rest."

"Let's scour the rows methodically, then. Look for her name, or if you can't make that out, check the date. It has to be 1875."

They moved away in opposite directions, and Amelia's face showed her disappointment when she rejoined her father under the tree-of-many-trunks after about forty minutes of searching. Each of them had covered an assigned area, but neither of them had cried out in discovery.

"Did you find any stone that might be hers?" Amelia asked without much hope.

"No, sorry, honey. . . . but what did you say was the name of her beau? Wasn't it Harold-something?"

Pah-rent moved away from the tree, striding to one of the worn markers. Amelia followed him.

"I noticed the name Harold here," he said as he gestured to the stone, "and the date is about right. If Muriel disappeared in 1875, when she was about 15, she'd have been born in 1860. If her boyfriend was, say 16, when she disappeared, he might have lived to be 65 or 70, if he wasn't taken in one of the wars or by a disease. So I'd say a Harold who died in—this marker says 1925—could be our man, if only we could verify his last name."

Amelia knelt by the stone and ran her fingers over the letters that still rose slightly from the limestone surface, and she felt a shiver of excitement run down her spine. Her fingers were "reading" the letters.

"Dad, I can make this out. W – E – L . . ." and the rest was entirely obliterated.

She raised eyes full of the wonder of discovery and whispered, "His name was Welch! The story named him. Harold Welch. Omigod, Dad, no Muriel, but here is Harold. We found him!"

"Eureka!" Pah-rent exclaimed.

19—HAL

"Pretty exciting, this research stuff, don't you think, Amelia?" Hal asked as they made their way down the hill, back toward the looming ocean.

The afternoon light was intense and nearly blinded them as it reflected off all that sea. His daughter had a new air about her, one of confidence. She seemed completely engaged in her project to help the ghost girl—he could hardly believe he was admitting the possibility—and she was directing their course of action.

"So we found Harold," Hal continued. "What do you think we ought to do next?"

"If I were to use the methods you've taught me all my life," Amelia began, "I'd have to say that not finding her grave does not necessarily lead to a certain conclusion." Amelia had taken on a lecturing tone of voice, half in jest, mimicking her impression of Hal talking, he guessed.

"If we are to discover what Muriel wants of us, we must try to share her vision of the world. We must try to know her experience and see through her eyes. I think we should proceed by following in her footsteps, visiting the places she might have seen and known."

Hal couldn't help smiling. He took this mimicry as a compliment to his own vocation and as a sign of a teasing affection.

"Well, certainly she had to eat sometime. Why don't we walk around in Nye Beach and get a bite ourselves? Suddenly I'm famished."

The Nye Beach area was the closest thing Newport had to a village. The streets were quaint—narrow and walkable—and there were still a few Victorian-style houses that had been kept up for a century or more. Sleek modern condos stood next to rows of dilapidated shacks with peeling paint, beach cabins that attested to this as a tourists' destination point all through the late 1800s and beyond.

In Muriel's day the streets were unpaved and the village itself a gathering of crude structures. In those days the beach sand was still used as a reliable highway—when the tide was out. But some of the Victorian homes had served as boarding houses, like the Burrows House that now sat on 9th Street near the Newport Armory, and one of these might have been Muriel's temporary home. They were in fact walking in Muriel's footsteps, just a cannon shot north of the lighthouse where she seemed stuck.

Hal and his daughter turned into one of the nautical cafés that lined the narrow street on the ocean side of the Nye Beach archway. First over chowder and then the fish and chips that followed, they discussed their plans.

"You know, in Muriel's time the real hub, the downtown of Newport as it were, was the bayfront," Hal began. "There was a small, chaotic settlement here in Nye Beach, but the real action was down along the bay where the boats docked. Remember, this is a great fishing port, still to this day. You and I saw the tall ships arrive, and that's where they're moored now, quite the colorful sight to remind us of an earlier era."

"Maybe that's where we should go next," Amelia replied. "It's harder than I anticipated to try to think like Muriel. Things have changed so greatly, and you have to imagine it all so much more—I don't know—rugged, I guess. Like a wild west town. And I'm not sure this is getting us any closer to her message for us, or what she wants us to do. Now that we're not so near the lighthouse, I don't feel her presence, or her urgency, quite as strong."

"Whenever you're ready to have your spine tingled and your hair curled again, we can always revisit the lighthouse and see what Muriel has in store for us," Hal reminded his daughter.

He realized he had begun to sound as if he were assuming Muriel was real—and ready to interact with them on a regular basis.

"If Muriel's been haunting that place for 140 years," he continued, "I wonder how many living folks she's tried to make contact with. I mean to say, doesn't it seem a little strange to you that she chose us? After you'd read her story and all—it seems like a weird coincidence."

"Maybe that's the very reason why," Amelia ventured after a slight pause. "I mean, that guide mentioned that other people had seen lights and felt her presence. But maybe they weren't receptive enough to actually see her or realize she's in need. I don't know, maybe it requires another girl, someone who's near her own age . . . someone who's also lost her mother! We might be just the right people she's been waiting for all these years! And Dad, I feel it as a kind of mission. I feel responsible for her, like if we don't help her, who will? When will she find the right conditions and get a chance to reach out again?"

"Well, even the scientific community recognizes that the universe may work by means of patterns and principles we're not aware of yet, honey. I'm impressed by the way you're thinking this through. And of course as always I love you for your heart. She reached out to you because you have such a great capacity to care about others."

Even though they'd been deeply wrapped up in their own conversation, Hal had noticed an elderly couple at a nearby table, and the woman had been staring at them off and on all through their meal. The couple got up to pay their bill, and the woman approached them tentatively with the man hanging back.

"Is that you, Amanda?" she said directly to Amelia.

Amelia looked inquiringly at Hal, obviously not knowing how to respond to the stranger's question.

"Um, I think you might have us confused with someone else," Hal said politely.

The woman squinted hard at Amelia again.

"Aren't you part of the Allen family?" she continued. "I could swear you're that Amanda all grown up that my granddaughter used to play with."

"Yes, that's our name," Hal replied with surprise, "but we're just visitors to Newport." He smiled, hoping to dismiss her. The man stepped up to join his wife.

"Well, my grandmother used to tell me this story. There was a fisherman, Allen by name, and he married up with a woman who'd come to town from California lookin' for that little gal who'd disappeared in the lighthouse."

Hal raised his eyes in wonder. The woman had his interest now, and Amelia was regarding her with curiosity.

"Oh, this was decades ago, in the olden times. She had a kind of Frenchy name, sister to that captain who'd dropped his daughter off here."

This was certainly Muriel's story. What an odd duck this woman was, with her thick-lensed glasses and an aura of frizzled silver hair.

"The French gal and this Allen had a son and a daughter as I recall, and that son carried on the family tradition of the fishing trade. There was a son from him too, who became harbor-master, and then as I recall another son after *he* got married, but that one went off to college, and I'm not sure what became of him."

With a sort of shock, it dawned on Hal that she meant *him.*

"That poor lost girl's father, he never came back, lost at sea himself, prolly, but the family line continued on in Newport through his sister. And your—daughter?—here," she put her hand on Hal's shoulder while her husband nodded vigorously, "is the spittin' image of the grand-daughter's daughter's daughter. . . . Wish I could remember that aunt's name. . . . My memory's not what it used to be. . . ."

Amelia looked up at the woman and found her voice.

"Was it Trevenard?"

"Nail on the head!" the woman shouted.

20—HAL

Sometimes in life we find something we weren't even looking for. This woman they'd never seen before had dropped a bomb out of the blue on them, just coincidentally, it seemed. But with this revelation so much of the eerie mystique of the last few days was falling into a sort of logic, even if it was still strange and magical—and rather unbelievable.

Hal had some sense of his own family tree, and he was proud of the fact that he came from a line of fishermen. It gave him a bit of credibility in his own profession. But he did not have a good memory for the maiden names of the women his male ancestors had married. For him growing up they had all simply been Allens—Grandma Allen, Greatgrandma Allen. He could remember that his grandparents had loved to use French phrases, and he had thought this odd for people from a laboring background. But it was one of those strange family tics you simply accepted. They wished a departing boat "*bon voyage*" and sea sickness was to them "*mal de mer*." And he'd been more than a little chagrined growing up that his own middle name was "Jean," pronounced like "John" but with a flair, more like "Zhahn." The other kids purposely mispronounced it. Their taunting chant still occasionally echoed in his ears, making him smile: "Harold Jean, can't be seen," and then they'd all cover their eyes.

His daughter had gone immediately to lie down after their café encounter with the woman, apparently in a kind of shock. Now Amelia walked back into the condo living room just as the shadows were beginning to lengthen over the bay.

Hal shook off his own reverie.

"Dad, I need to talk to you!" his daughter implored. "I think I'm confused, but maybe not. Maybe everything's getting clear all of a sudden. Can you help me understand what that strange woman said? And what she meant by it?"

"It was kind of a jolt having her recognize us like that," Hal replied. "She seems to have lived in Newport all her life, and she certainly thought you looked like a girl she knew. Of course, she was mistaking you for someone else," he added comfortingly.

"But who, Dad? How did she know our name was Allen?"

"I've been thinking about that, honey. You know, Uncle Jim and Aunt Sally have often taken their vacation here, just like we do. I wonder if that woman's grand-daughter might have played with your cousin Amanda at some point. The two of you do share a family resemblance, and the lady might have a very good eye for faces."

Amelia stared out at the reds and yellows of the setting sun now reflected in the bay, and she couldn't keep her eyes off the lighthouse, which sat placidly in the late afternoon glitter across the water. She wondered if Muriel was looking back at her from behind the mirrored windows. She felt a connection to the ghost girl she just could not shake off. An unvoiced question sat between Amelia and her father almost like a third person in the room with them.

"Is that story she told about the fisherman marrying a French lady true?" she finally asked.

"I don't remember all their last names . . . but it sounds plausible to me," Hal said hesitatingly as his voice trailed off.

Amelia responded slowly and clearly: "And that fisherman was our family? . . . So, Muriel's aunt Trevenard—her father's sister—is your great-great-grandmother? And my great-great-great grand-mother?" She looked him directly in the eyes.

"It would seem so."

He marveled at his own admission, trying to downplay his daughter's sense of the great drama of the moment.

Amelia doubled over and clutched at her stomach.

"Dad, everything's churning inside me. It's all coming together. Muriel has been waiting for her family to come and rescue her. It's too late for her father, many years too late, but we have finally arrived. And she recognized us. And reached out to us. Who knows what kind of effort this was for her? She's totally real."

Hal rose and put his arm around Amelia, who seemed on the verge of nausea.

"Do you need a drink of water, honey?"

Amelia straightened up and took a deep breath.

"And now we have to help her. We've got to get her out of that lighthouse and put to rest. She needs to be up there on the hill next to Harold. And I'm going to figure out how to make it happen."

21—Muriel

The endless routine of the lighthouse had returned. Muriel shrouded herself away by day as tourists tromped through the house, some even approaching her hidden cupboard at the top of the spiral stairs. And by night she made a mark on the wall and lit her light in the tower ever so briefly.

She retained a small sense of the excited hope that had animated her when she reached out to the girl who so resembled a modern version of herself, and to the girl's protective father. Her heart ached when she remembered his gentle concern for his daughter, the way he cradled her shoulders in his arm. To her way of thinking, these two were a perfect image of Muriel and her own father. But was there more to their attraction for her?

Over the decades, after fully realizing her condition and her predicament—and the physics of living as a ghost—Muriel had occasionally tried to make contact with a seemingly sympathetic visitor. If someone paused near her, perhaps sensing her presence, Muriel had focused her energy and her will to make the person see her clearly.

This attempt had garnered varied results. At times the individual acted uneasy but continued to look right through her. Sometimes the person would startle, eyes wide, and beat a hasty path to the front door. Once she'd tried to materialize to a young girl, who seemed to see her and put out her arms, waving them right through Muriel's body—then simply giggled and ran away.

At these times Muriel felt like the lighthouse freak attraction. If no one took her seriously, then how could she ask for help? Her other, usual, options had borne no results, either. She sometimes, out of frustration, cried "Help me! Help me! Help me!" yet no one answered her call. And although a sense of futility and despair had nearly overcome her, she still sent out her little light from the tower on a dark night.

That night before she had reached out to the man and his daughter, Muriel thought she saw a light answering her own from across the bay. At its slight glimmer, she had focused her intention over the water to its source. And in her mind's eye she'd had a brief vision of a man's face, that same face that had appeared the next day at the foot of the stairs to her house. In her brief flash of him the night before she had sensed a hurt like her own, a kind of kinship of loss.

When he appeared with his daughter she felt even more drawn to them. That girl seemed so much like Muriel herself. It was not just that they were a father and daughter bereft of a mother. Muriel sensed a familiarity—and an openness—in them, almost as if they were distant cousins, part of her own family.

She was certain the man had seen her at the window as they approached. And then the girl had appeared without hesitation at the door of her cupboard. They'd seemed to sense her aura when she stood near them, and so she'd once again focused all her being to show them her earthly image. The girl had seen Muriel's reflection as hoped—and yet she had not fled nor cursed her as a devilish vision.

Muriel held a certainty that she had communicated her need for help across time boundaries to a young woman who even now, in the twenty-first century, so resembled the young girl who'd gone back to the lighthouse to find her handkerchief but instead had lost herself to the future. And now she had to trust them, daughter and father, to find her release from her prison and a final resting place. Perhaps it was not even too much to hope that somehow she could find peace near to dear Harold, whom she still held close to her heart.

22—AMELIA

Amelia had a restless night. She couldn't get the vision of Muriel's face floating in the lighthouse window out of her mind. And she was agitated, unsure of what to do next. All Amelia knew was that she must help this poor lost ghost girl, her ancestor, find some peace.

Several times through the night she rose and peered across the dark bay at the light-house. In the dim light of a crescent moon it even looked like it held an untold secret. The eyes of the windows gazed right back at her and then, toward morning— had she imagined it?—she thought she saw a feeble signal glimmering in the tower. Amelia equated this to Muriel's own spirit, weakening, finding no help over all these years. Amelia blinked, and then the light was gone.

She still wanted to see Newport through Muriel's eyes if she could. When Pah-rent suggested breakfast on the bayfront, she agreed quickly, hoping that place might offer her some insight. As soon as they got out of the car the sounds of the bay overcame them: constant barking of sea lions, a whooshing wind pushing upriver from the ocean, and the clanging of the harbor buoys as they bobbed with the choppiness of the tides.

The streets held a motley arrangement of canneries and shops, with casual eateries interspersed. Many displayed colorful wood signs painted with mermaids or anchors, and store windows were crowded with nautical items like glass floats and thick ropes on huge spools. They walked along upriver on a side-walk that became a boardwalk running along the ramps leading down to the berths of fishing vessels.

She smiled upon recognizing the complicated masts and beams of the *Hawaiian Chieftain*, her magical tall ship now with sails stored away neatly—and looking rather out of place moored among the sleeker more modern boats. She could see now that the crew still bustling aboard the craft wore authentic nineteenth-century garb. This ship might be similar, she thought, to the pirate vessel that shanghaied Muriel's mother—her own ancestor as they had now confirmed.

Far different from what she had expected from summer vacation, one thing this adventure was showing her was how she lived in a web of interconnection. Just last year, as a fourteen-year-old, she couldn't see beyond the details of her school day—who texted who, what her friends were wearing, the latest pop song. Now she was beginning to see that others she paid little attention to were invested in her being. That lady at the café had recognized her simply because of her heritage. Lives of people who'd walked this boardwalk in the past had given a shape and a direction to her own life path.

Everyday decisions sometimes felt overwhelming and super important to her. But now she saw that maybe there was a larger force directing the shape of her future. Maybe her actions weren't always by choice. Maybe you could just be who you were in the right place at the right time, regardless of what you thought you wanted. Running into someone by chance or being witness to an unusual event—if you could connect the dots, these might draw a clear picture you hadn't seen before, sort of like the faces of animals hidden in a painting. Once those shapes popped into view, you wondered how you'd missed seeing them all along.

Amelia turned her eyes toward the shops on the land side of the bay road. The earthy aroma of coffee had wafted toward them, and Pah-rent had taken her arm to steer her toward its source. A small shop next door to the café with a neon sign just starting to flash "OPEN" caught her attention. Its sign read "Psychic Messages" and in very small type on the door, "from the other side."

Pah-rent nudged Amelia toward the coffee shop door, but on a whim she veered left and pushed open the psychic's door. Incense smoke hung in the air like heavy fog. A little bell tinkled as they entered, and a woman with long dark hair came out from behind a curtain of beads, which clattered as she shouldered them aside. The shop was small and cluttered with shelves holding bright candles and odd talismans—miniature figurines, macabre skulls and bones, and packets of herbal mixtures. A tiny table sat to one side, containing only a large crystal ball on a stand, and a deck of tarot cards.

The woman eyed Amelia and her father carefully, as if sizing them up. Amelia smiled at her tentatively.

"You seek a message from the other side?" the woman said. "I am Fatima."

She placed a finger on her temple and rolled her eyes toward the ceiling.

"I see a third figure, a woman, walking with you. This is a loved one you have lost?"

Amelia gulped hard, then replied, "Well, yes, but that's not why we're here. Have you ever helped release a spirit that needs to be laid to rest?"

"Come, sit," Fatima said, and gestured toward the tiny table.

Amelia turned to look at Pah-rent, who seemed awkward and uncomfortable in these stuffy and cramped quarters. Fatima produced a third chair, and they clustered around her table. The seer bent over and retrieved a credit card reader, which she laid on the table, then sat with both palms flat before her, looking Amelia directly in the face.

"This restless spirit, it disturbs you?" Fatima asked.

"Not really, not the way you mean," Amelia began. "But she's a girl, my ancestor, who got trapped, and we need to help lay her to rest."

"She haunts in your house?" Fatima pursued.

"No, not our house. The Yaquina Bay Lighthouse just up at the mouth of the bay." Amelia gestured west.

"This is where she lived?"

"No, she was just sight-seeing there, and she disappeared. Only drops of blood remained of her."

"You mean spirit who is lighthouse ghost," Fatima said matter-of-factly. "Long time she walks there."

Pah-rent shifted in his chair impatiently. He seemed like a giant stuck in a dollhouse.

"You have remains?" Fatima still didn't quite get the picture.

"No one knows about that," Amelia persisted. "Her ghost is what remains, trapped in the house. She needs to be released and laid to rest. Can you help us set her free?"

Fatima sat quietly with her eyes closed, almost as if in a trance. Pah-rent touched Amelia on the shoulder and started to rise from his chair.

Fatima's eyes slitted open, and she said quickly, "Stay. Sit. . . . I will help. For the daughter it is important. And for this you will need to find some piece of the ghost's earthly form. With this we can draw her spirit forth and remove her from the house."

Pah-rent spoke at last. "A piece of her earthly form . . . do you mean, some part of her body?"

"Yes, even a small fragment of bone will do it." Fatima extended her palm. "And that will be $20, Papa."

23—Hal

He didn't exactly regret having given Amelia free rein in her project, but now Hal was faced with a sticky situation. Amelia would not let go of the idea that they needed to find a "piece" of Muriel, and that posed a challenge. Over fourteen decades no remains had been located that they knew of, and where would one look, anyway? The disappearance of the young girl was still a mystery. Hal knew the lighthouse had been repaired and restored. If something was lodged in the walls, it would have emerged then. And this was state property. He knew they couldn't just poke around, no matter their intentions. Yet his daughter was determined to save Muriel and get her relocated to the cemetery.

It also did not escape Hal that now he was giving full credibility to the existence of a ghost, and that they were embarking on a task that his rational mind saw as dubious at best. Could he now put a stop to what might be nonsense? The parent in him said no. He'd agreed to give Amelia autonomy in this project, and he couldn't back out on their bargain at this advanced stage. But he wondered if he was, through sentiment for Amelia, giving into craziness or folly. He felt pulled into a child's vision of reality. And now they would follow through with public actions.

Before he would allow her to shovel around on the lighthouse grounds, Hal knew he needed to check with the authorities. There was a garden-area at the back of the house, and he didn't want Amelia digging willy-nilly in there, risking arrest. Hal called the park system and got the number for the lighthouse curator. She would meet him behind the lighthouse near the storage shed. And he knew his daughter needed to be part of the conversation.

Behind the lighthouse Hal and Amelia spotted the low outbuildings that serviced the park. A woman in a dark khaki uniform saw them and waved. Her I.D. tag read Letitia Bonaparte. She confirmed this by extending her hand.

"Dr. Allen? Letty Bonaparte," she offered. "And this must be . . .?"

"My daughter Amelia."

"Nice to meet you both! How can I help you?"

As she smiled in greeting, Letitia Bonaparte's teeth flashed brightly, and Hal was momentarily struck by the comic but strangely appealing image of her short dreadlocks as they escaped from her ranger's cap and pointed in every direction.

He exchanged a glance with Amelia and decided to try tact in broaching the topic.

"This may sound a bit out of the ballpark, but are you familiar with the legend of the ghost that haunts the lighthouse?"

Letty raised her eyebrows.

"Sure, we've all heard the story. Muriel—girl who disappeared here back in the 1800s, just after the light was abandoned."

Hal was considering what to say next when Amelia took over.

"Have you seen the ghost?"

"Sweetie, I'm a park ranger, but I'm a scientist too," Letty smiled at her. "My job is physical artifacts and preservation of the past. I leave what goes on in the spirit world to others."

Hal picked up the inquiry as Letty seemed more of his mind set despite those wayward braids.

"As we understand it, her body was never found. We were wondering, during the reconstruction, were there any excavations?"

"Oh, yes!" Letty warmed to her subject. "This area is rich in buried history. First, there are native artifacts—here we found a small midden of oyster shells and various tools shaped out of bone. Then of course fishermen from the early days of settlement left their traces too. We've dug up lots of fish spines and fragments of boating equipment. Most of these are just bits and pieces. Wood doesn't hold up too well in the wet ground."

"Where were the excavations?" Hal asked.

"These were found right along the back of the house here inside the foundation, just beyond that garden."

"Inside the boundaries of the house itself, hmmm? Was there any sign of a . . . tunnel or cave? I know that's an odd question."

"Funny you should ask. There is a shaft that descends from the room at the top of the spiral stairs. We've closed it off for safety."

"And in all this digging, no trace of what might be Muriel?"

A darkness came over Letty's eyes.

"Why are you so interested? Our artifacts are off-limits, I'm afraid, to spook-hunters and treasure-seekers."

"I understand your concern," Hal assured her, "but we're, well, we're Muriel's relatives. My daughter here has made it her personal mission to have our ancestor properly commemorated at the cemetery. And if there are possibly any remains, we'd like to claim them."

Letty dropped her guard at this and said, "Yes, we would certainly allow that if you can show proof of relation. I myself was not in charge of the dig as it was in 1974, and I've spent only the last six months sorting through the old labeled baggies and cataloguing the items. Shall we take a look at the collection?"

Hal liked this woman's direct manner, and he returned her gaze steadily.

"I can bring in our family tree to show you how Muriel's aunt was my great-great-grandmother," he offered.

"That should do it."

As they moved toward the shed, Letty asked Amelia, "Do you enjoy science classes in school? When I was growing up, they encouraged girls to study arts and home ec. But I always loved the lab. It was *my* kitchen."

"We haven't done much yet except look at amoebas and dissect frogs, which was kind of yucky," Amelia responded freely. "I prefer to draw. But I do like learning how things work, and how it all fits together into some sort of system. Genus, family, species, and evolution and all that kind of stuff."

"I have to confess I love digging up traces of the past," Letty continued. "My mom encouraged me to follow my own heart. And where's your mom today? Doesn't she share your interest?"

"My mom died in January," Amelia replied softly.

Letty placed her arm around Amelia's shoulder without a word and lifted her eyes to Hal's face.

"Oh . . . I kind of know how you must feel. I lost my dad when I was young," Letty volunteered.

"You did?"

"It was so hard to go on—and I still miss him," she added.

When they reached the shed door, Letty dropped her arm and unlocked the padlock. Amelia reached into her backpack and pulled out her sketchbook.

"Here, Letty, here's a drawing I made of Mom."

"She looks beautiful, sweetie. I see that you resemble her. And who's this?" Letty asked, pointing to a girl's face drawn on the opposite page. "Do you have a sister?"

"That," Amelia pronounced dramatically, "is Muriel, the lighthouse ghost!"

"Well, I know the story, but I don't think I've ever seen a depiction of her before. Did you make this out of your imagination?"

"No, I drew this after we saw her in the front hall. Her face appeared just behind mine reflected in the window. And I think I caught it pretty well, don't you agree, Dad?"

Amelia looked up at her father, but Letty abruptly turned back to the lock on the shed and removed it, pulling open the door.

"You saw the ghost, eh?" she smiled.

They all stepped into the shed, and she snapped on the lights, low-hanging rectangular fluorescent fixtures over long tables with small compartments. Baggies filled these compartments, some of which were carefully labeled with hand-printed cards.

"This is our storehouse for any artifacts found on the grounds," Letty explained. "The sections are sorted out into type of artifact. The ones with labels have been catalogued. Each baggie has a number within its section and a full description on another card in our files. Eventually I'll enter all the data into the computer, but for now we're still sorting. I haven't even begun the 'Human Remains' sector yet. Ah, here it is."

She picked up a small notebook and scanned the entries.

"The excavation team kept notes as they removed items, indicating exact location and any suggested interpretation. I see here," and she placed her head very near to Hal's so he could see the writing, "that there are pieces of human bone."

She moved her finger to a line of script, brushing Hal's hand in the process. Together they bent their heads over the small notebook, both reading silently. Amelia stepped toward them.

"Dad?"

"This is a full description of the discovery and the protocol," he said. "The excavation team had invited up the sheriff's office, it says here, and they sent over a forensics expert from Corvallis to examine the bones. There was a skeleton, almost entirely intact . . . and they identified it as a teen-aged female!"

He looked excitedly at his daughter.

"There was trauma to the skull consistent with a fall," he continued reading, "and it had been in the ground between 100 and 150 years. No certain identification could be made, and they ruled out foul play that would relate to any of their cold cases."

"I remember hearing that all the police records prior to 1920 had been destroyed in a fire when the station burned," Letty added.

Hal picked up reading: "They removed the skeleton . . ."

"They took her bones away?" Amelia groaned.

". . . which slightly disintegrated upon full excavation. Remaining bone fragments were bagged by the museum and kept in the collection."

Letty reached into the compartment and pulled out a large plastic bag holding a small, flat, weathered bone fragment.

She held it up and exclaimed, "I think we just may have found your girl! . . . But the evidence is all terribly circumstantial. I can't with certainty say these are Muriel's remains."

She replaced the baggie in the bin.

"But they have to be!" Amelia said passionately. "Who else would be a teen-age girl who fell down the shaft exactly the time Muriel disappeared?"

Hal intervened.

"Letty, Amelia's just adding up the clues, and it's as scientific as we can get with the evidence we have. The pieces don't make a complete picture, but by the process of elimination it seems all arrows are pointing to Muriel. We don't need all the fragments. Just a bit or two, and we can lay our ancestor to rest. Your collection won't miss one small section of bone."

"Please?" Amelia added.

"Well, you're right. I guess one small specimen won't damage the archives. Bring me that paperwork, and we can sign this fragment over to you."

Letty smiled warmly at Hal as he handed back the book, and she declared, "May your Muriel rest in peace at last!"

24—AMELIA

Pah-rent had followed through on the paper-work to acquire Muriel's bone by taking in their family tree, and Amelia was full of the thrill of expectation. It seemed strange that he needed to have so many meetings with Ms. Letty, and the days of making arrangements were filled with long absences, leaving Amelia alone in the condo.

She was restless and eager to rescue Muriel. She tried to imagine what would come next. She knew that she could get near to the ghost by approaching the spot of the iron door up the spiral stairs. And she could take the bone fragment along with her, but then what? She was sure that simply burying the bone would not free Muriel. Somehow she had to unite the ghostly spirit with her earthly remains.

This morning she'd found a note on the kitchen table next to Muriel's bone: "Gone to meet with Letty about finishing up the bone papers. Back this afternoon, Dad." Sometimes adults got awfully distracted, it seemed. Here was the bone, and just across the bay was Muriel in distress. *I'm just going to have to handle this myself,* Amelia decided. She was sure that Fatima would know how to connect the ghost with her earthly remains, and the shop was not a long walk away.

It was a sunny day; the waters of the bay sparkled with light. Amelia tucked the bone-bag into her backpack and walked over to the bridge, turning right rather than left toward the lighthouse at its north end, and circled down past the Coast Guard station to the bayfront. This was beginning to seem like familiar territory to her. She ambled past the canneries, restaurants, and shops, dodging the foot traffic of tourists who looked to be from all around the world. There were snatches of Spanish and other languages she could not recognize, and, as always, the barks of the resident sea lions.

The air smelled briny and fishy as she turned down the dock to look at the floating platforms the animals had taken over. They were enormous and sort of glossy in the morning light, each claiming a lounging spot on the wood planks. If another sea lion tried to slide onto the same platform, the resident would bark furiously, defending his space as home territory.

Even animals need a sense of place, Amelia mused as she stood along the railing with people who each had a special spot in the world to call theirs. And that's what Muriel needed too. It was your family and loved ones who made you feel at home, and then you needed to be established in a place that was no one else's. Muriel had been a perpetual visitor in the lighthouse all these years. Now it was up to her family to get her situated in her personal space, home next to Harold.

Amelia felt the presence of the bone in her pack and returned to her mission of the day, walking up the boardwalk to the psychic's shop. All was just as it had been before. The "OPEN" light flashed on as Amelia crossed the street toward it, and the bell jingled as she pushed at the door, entering the room filled with the expected incense fog. She'd purposely put a $20 bill in her jeans pocket, and she was willing to pay if Fatima could tell her what to do next.

The bead curtain whooshed aside, and there stood Fatima.

"You seek to know the future?" she asked without looking up, then, brushing her long hair aside, "Ah, the little girl but without her papa! Let me see, the bone, the bone. Do you have the bone?"

Fatima moved to her seat at the small table. Amelia sat across from her and rummaged in her pack, pulling out the sealed plastic bag containing a fragment of Muriel. She placed this proudly on the table between them.

Fatima seemed surprised as she regarded the package.

"Do you need to do something to it?" Amelia prompted. "Say some words or something? And what am I supposed to do next? Is there some kind of ritual?"

"Do you have money? Money for information."

Fatima patted her palm on the table. Amelia dug the $20 out of her pocket and laid it on the spot. It disappeared immediately through some sleight of hand, and Fatima put her fingers to her temples, rolling her eyes toward the ceiling. A low hum sort of like "Ohmmm" vibrated the table.

At last Fatima opened her eyes.

"You wish to remove spirit from house to graveyard, yes?"

Amelia nodded.

"So, I will give you the spirit-spray. This you must wear like a cologne, all over your clothes. No others can detect smell, but spirit it will attract to you. You must do this alone. Take bone to place of spirit and hold it forth in both hands. The important part here it comes. You must close eyes and think only of light. Bring image of this person into your mind. You must say words—what is spirit name?"

"Muriel."

"You must say, 'Muriel, I mean you no harm. I am your vessel. I hold forth your remains. Come into me, and I will take you to your resting place.' Hold her image still in your mind then breathe like this: short short short out, long and deep in, into your belly. Do this three times—but no more than three!—or you might be harmed by wandering bad spirit."

"Out out out, then in deep, the whole thing three times, got it."

"But no more than three! Very dangerous! The third time take breath so deep you almost blow up.

You will feel something move inside. You make room for spirit. Then you go directly to graveyard. Bury bone. Stand over grave and say prayer: 'Muriel, here you are laid to rest. God keep you in his eternal peace.' Make deep breath out from belly. And she will be free."

Fatima reached behind her and brought forward an atomizer, which she placed on the table next to the bone.

"Wash clothes when done or you may attract unwanted spirit," she warned. "And now Fatima must rest. May God bless you in your deed, and think only of light!" Fatima dropped her head and slumped over the table.

Amelia picked up the bone and the spray, situating them in her backpack, and then pulled open the shop door to Newport bay's clear air and blinding sunlight.

25—MURIEL

She couldn't put her finger on any reason in particular, but Muriel felt a change a-coming. Some nights, as she peered from the tower sending out her own feeble beam, she was certain that the light across the bay was an answer to her own—and a promise. After decades of an increasing sense of isolation and abandonment, Muriel had come to feel even more than orphaned, completely friendless. But discovering this daughter—this modern version of herself—and her concerned father had given Muriel hope again. With them she remembered the possibility of family. With their apparent openness to her existence and her plight, she felt real again and almost whole.

But did they fully understand her need for release? Had she gotten the message through to them that she needed help?

Muriel had become accustomed to the changing faces of khaki-clad rangers who worked through and around the lighthouse. Along with the tourists they walked up and down the stairs and hustled through the hallways. None of them had seemed to sense her in particular. Once she had tried to materialize to one of the guides just as he was talking to a family of tourists about the myth of a lighthouse ghost. She had stood toward the rear of the family group and concentrated to make herself apparent.

In retrospect she found this episode kind of amusing. The guide had slowly become aware of her, a pale spectral face lurking behind the vibrant parents and children. She had not meant her appearance as ironic, but so it was. She saw the guide's eyes pass over her, then return. He blinked and made an obvious attempt to process what he thought he saw, just as he was pronouncing her haunting as "the product of an overactive imagination." Before he could respond to this vision of her, she disappeared.

The memory gave Muriel a quick smile, but its deeper truth was still tragic. She was trapped; she was terribly alone; and she was, so far over all these years, helpless and friendless.

Light footsteps and soft laughter outside her cupboard broke Muriel out of her reverie. Her first thought was of tourists, and she generally remained still until they moved on. This time she recognized the two voices, a man and a woman. Muriel rose and stepped onto the landing to investigate, nearly colliding with a ranger she recognized and, wonder of wonders, the modern girl's father!

"Yes, we've been up here before," the father was saying as he guided the ranger by holding her arm. "This is where Amelia felt a coldness move out toward us from the wall."

"The iron door opened right here to a shaft that descended straight down," the guide responded. "Here."

She took the father's hand in her own and placed it against the wall. Their eyes met, and they smiled at each other.

Muriel stood less than a foot away, eavesdropping. This was not, she thought, a good moment to materialize. Nothing would be gained.

"Oh, yes, I can see then how those bones would have been deposited very near the foundation if someone had fallen down the shaft," the father remarked.

Muriel examined his face closely, noting how much the daughter resembled her father. He seemed a gentle person in demeanor, even kind. She wondered why the girl was not with him.

"But tell me, Letty, do you feel a kind of chill in the air right now?" He put out his hand. "Warmer here, but cool, right here."

He took Letty's hand and guided it to the cool spot, very near to Muriel. And then they stood, still holding hands, the woman looking flustered, the color rising in her cheeks—just as Muriel herself had felt in receiving Harold's attentions.

The guide blurted something out to mask her embarrassment: "Why did it take you so long to lay claim to Muriel's remains?"

"We didn't realize this lost girl was a relative of ours until a chance meeting with a local woman who recognized us as part of the Trevenard line," the father responded.

Muriel felt stunned at hearing her own last name, and she lurched sideways toward the wall, nearly brushing right through the woman, who shivered.

"And now it does seem our responsibility to make sure her remains are relocated to a dignified resting place," he continued to an audience of a giddy park ranger and a stupefied ghost. "Her life ended in a tragedy, poor dear, and we don't want her death to end up the same way."

"I fully understand," Letty said, reclaiming her composure. "Sometimes we underestimate the importance of family, especially shirt-tail relations. I'm not sure I believe in ghosts, but I do feel the chill right here by the old door. You should always be able to rely on your family. Always. I admire you and your daughter for taking on this task."

Muriel continued to lean against the wall. Her knees felt weak.

The couple turned to descend the stairs, Hal keeping his hold on Letty to help steady her.

"We assume ghosts want release," he was saying. "But if they do 'exist' somehow, I wonder how they experience being laid to rest. What change in consciousness would this bring to a ghost? I guess we'll never know. . . ."

His voice trailed off as they moved down the stairs, leaving Muriel alone in wonder on the landing.

For taking on this task, the woman had said. *The importance of family*, she had said. . . . By some miracle they are my relatives, my own family! Muriel realized as it all sank in. They called out to me; I reached out to them. And at last they have returned to rescue me.

In her excitement she did not even consider the changes for herself that might lie ahead.

26—HAL

Hal returned to the condo filled with an unaccustomed glow of anticipation and excitement, which had virtually nothing to do with the lighthouse ghost. The source of his happiness was an earnest park ranger to whom he had taken immediately. As he had contrived reasons to meet with her about Muriel's bones over the past several days, he'd found his attraction growing even stronger, and Letty seemed to return his interest. He had rediscovered the thrill of flirtation—inadvertent touches, confidential smiles and gazes, teasing remarks.

After Gillian's death Hal had been certain he could never love like that again. Such love inevitably leads to loss, he had felt, and who would willingly put himself through such suffering? Yet here he was, his heart warming inside him, ready to risk all once again. He took this as a very good sign.

His note sat on the table where he'd left it, but he noticed that the bone was gone, and so was his daughter. He'd hardly had time to worry about this when the condo door slammed.

"There you are, Dad. Boy, do I have news."

Amelia shrugged off her backpack and replaced the bone onto the table, along with a strange-looking atomizer bottle.

"What have you got there? And where have you been, missy?" he said, trying to act stern.

"You'd done your disappearing act again," Amelia responded, "so since we have the bone I visited Fatima to find out what to do next. I have the plan, Dad. And Fatima says I must do it alone. I need you to help me decide when the time is right. I'm thinking the sooner the better. Do we need to get Letty's permission?"

"I'm sure I can take care of that," Hal replied. "But I'm not sold on setting you loose in the lighthouse to perform some mumbo-jumbo. I'm not convinced of Fatima's authority in such matters."

"You do believe in Muriel, don't you?"

Hal paused.

"You saw her, Dad, in the window," Amelia prompted.

"Yes, against all that I know rationally, I saw that face," he admitted.

"And you recognized her face in my drawing! There's no other choice but moving ahead to set her free. How could we live with ourselves if we turned our backs? Fatima's plan is really our only option, Dad, unless you can think of something more scientific."

"*Touché*, my practical daughter. Strange circumstances may require strange remedies. What exactly does Fatima recommend?"

"I'm forbidden to tell you the details."

Hal frowned.

"But it's easy, and I won't be in danger. I will carry Muriel's spirit out of the lighthouse, and I'll need you to drive us to the graveyard fast. . . . Can you put a shovel in the car? And Dad? Can we nail together a wooden cross, or something holy to sanctify her place of rest? We can bury her bone next to Harold's grave and mark the spot with the cross."

Hal mentally went over the layout of the cemetery. Amelia's plan was emotionally strong, but what about the mundane details? He knew that mourners embellished grave sites all the time. They'd seen someone planting a flower bush there, and all kinds of crosses and flags had been staked into the ground near gravestones. If they kept the bone fragment sealed up in its baggie, all would be legit, he thought. A cross would not be at all out of place.

"Dad? Can you get the cross?"

"There are some leftover pieces of wood down in the storage area," Hal said. "I'm sure we can nail together something rudimentary. But I'm still not keen on leaving you alone in that house."

"You'll be right outside waiting for me—and the guides will be downstairs in the dining room. If we go first thing in the morning, no tourists will be there yet. I'll use the bone to attract her spirit, and we'll get her to the graveyard where she belongs. And Dad? Can we do it tomorrow? I've got Fatima's words fresh in my mind . . . and I know Muriel is anxious."

*   *   *

Hal found two pieces of wood, one slightly longer than the other, in the stack at the back of the parking garage. There was a small hammer in the condo but no nails at all. Almost as if by instinct or some sort of gravitational pull he tucked the wood under his arm and walked across the bridge to the lighthouse. He climbed the stairs toward the house but veered around to the back. The door to the shed was open, and Letty was concentrating on one of the bins.

Hal leaned his wood outside the door and tiptoed in until he was right behind Letty. He encircled her with his arms from behind, and she let out a little shriek of surprise, then turned and answered his embrace with a warm one of her own.

"Can't you see I'm hard at work?" she chastised playfully.

"I was just sure you needed my help," he responded in kind. "I heard you calling out to me from across the bay, a little voice saying 'Help me!' And so, after dashing across the bridge to your side, here I am, your savior."

He kissed Letty impulsively.

"Are you saving me or distracting me?" she laughed.

"Actually, my dove, I need *your* help today."

He disentangled himself and fetched the pieces of wood.

"My daughter is bent upon following through some kind of ritual given to her by the resident psychic. She plans to 'transport' the spirit of your lighthouse ghost to the cemetery—tomorrow morning, mind you—and we are to install her there with a cross." He held up the two pieces of wood. "I'm in need of a hammer and nails. Can the state of Oregon assist one of its former citizens—even though she's now a ghost—in marking her final resting place?"

Letty quickly moved to a workbench at the back of the shed and Hal followed. She routed out a small indentation in the crosspiece and fitted it onto the upright. Then she held the piece in place while Hal toenailed in three long brads to hold it securely.

"*Voilá*," she said, holding up the rustic-looking cross. "Courtesy of your park service."

"I'm sure Amelia will be pleased. The things we parents go through . . ."

"So, tomorrow morning? What does Miss Amelia intend to do?"

"She won't tell. Fatima has sworn her to secrecy. I'm to wait in the car for a quick getaway to the cemetery with Muriel along with us."

"And me," Letty added.

"And the cross. But you don't need to participate, really, Letty. I'm doing it to make my daughter happy. Yet I maintain my skepticism about the entire project."

Letty set down the cross and took both of Hal's hands in her own.

"Listen, I know our friendship is very new, and I don't mean to presume. But I've already realized that this thing we have between us is larger than just a quick summer flirtation. I've already come to care about what's best for both you and Amelia. And looking at the ghost situation from the outside, knowing she's your ancestor and all, I can tell you that this task is important for Amelia, but also in your own life, in getting you through your grief."

Hal's eyes teared up slightly, and Letty squeezed his hands.

"My own family comes originally from Guadeloupe and we have a saying, 'You are the strand that makes the twine strong.' Without being woven into the braid, each of us is weak and puny. But when we realize that the twine begins somewhere and goes on indefinitely into the future, we see our place in the whole string of our family. Without each individual, the rope weakens. Yet the separate strands connect and intertwine, and when we perform our duty we keep it going. We come from the past and make a way for others down the line."

"Metaphors aren't really my thing, but I see what you're saying. With Gillian's death I've sort of given up on the future. But ironically this Muriel business launches Amelia and maybe even myself forward, by dealing with the past."

"Not everything can be explained scientifically," Letty added. "You've done a good thing in letting Amelia see this as her personal mission. Whatever kind of ritual she wants to perform, and whether there actually is a ghost-Muriel or not, what matters is the effect on your daughter. Let her have her success—and help her as you can. That's why I want to be in on it too. Putting Muriel to rest is the way both of you are stepping away from your grief and your loss."

"Wise words, my friend. I do appreciate your advice. I'll do my best for Amelia's sake. And dear Letty, I hope you will be there too."

"How could I not?" She released his hands and reached for the cross. "I'll be ready at opening time tomorrow."

Hal took the newly-made marker and, leaning over it, gave Letty a quick kiss. He hoisted the cross awkwardly onto his shoulder, and he set off to traverse the Yaquina Bay Bridge, back to the condo.

"How strange a sight I must be, a man on foot bearing a very large cross," he thought, as his figure was silhouetted against the ocean's reflected brightness, a father, on a mission, for his daughter and for himself.

27–Amelia

Her heart jolted. She had gone to the window to peer across at the lighthouse. Amelia did this now several times a day, and into the night hours she searched for a feeble light in the tower—a sure sign of Muriel, and of Amelia's duty. But now, nothing but the placid lighthouse windows reflecting the sky and the waters of the bay. Her eyes had wandered upriver to the bridge. A small figure was laboring toward the mid-rise, and on its shoulders sat a large cross, bobbing up and down with each pace.

This could only be Pah-rent, and his image brightened the now-familiar sight of the Conde McCullough bridge. He'd followed through for her; he'd gotten the bone and now the cross. Amelia herself had the spirit-spray and the ritualistic words. As she waited for Pah-rent's descent off the bridge and back to the condo, Amelia chuckled at how much she'd grown up in the past few weeks. Not long ago she'd been languishing in misery, missing her school chums. Now she saw that life flowed on even away from the big city. Pah-rent had been right: if you opened yourself up to where you were, things you never expected might fall right onto your path. Mom had a favorite saying, "Bloom where you're planted." Ironically, this Newport she'd so dreaded for the summer was a place Amelia'd begun to find a sense of her true self.

Amelia turned at the sound of the door closing. Pah-rent faced her, cross-less, breathing hard. Small beads of sweat glistened on his brow.

"I saw you on the bridge!" Amelia greeted him.

"Then you saw the cross, too. People were honking and waving as I walked over. I guess I was quite the spectacle."

Hal sat down on the sofa.

"Is everything cleared with Letty? For tomorrow?" Amelia asked from her chair near the window. "I think this will be Muriel's last night as a prisoner if all goes as Fatima said it will."

"We will give Madame Fatima's plan an honest attempt, honey. I'll be in the car with the cross, and with Letty too. You take care of your part, and we'll get you up to the cemetery to complete the burial. . . .What an unexpected summer adventure we're having, my grown-up daughter! And you thought nothing could go on without your cell phone."

"Dad? . . . You sure have been spending a lot of time over in the shed with Letty."

"Well, she's been very helpful in getting things set up for your ritual. We need to make sure we work within the boundaries of public agencies' regulations. What we have here is an unusual situation."

"Do you like her, Dad?"

"We have a lot in common, Amelia, and I do find her intriguing."

"I really like her," Amelia ventured. "She's so easy to talk to, and I love her smile and that funny hair-do. I wonder if she could help me put braids like that in my hair."

Amelia began pulling and twisting strands near her face. Some of her best memories had to do with the gentle pulling and tugging of her hair as Mom tried to make neat, long braids for her. Letty's short, choppy dreadlocks seemed so modern by comparison.

"Could we ask her over to the condo for dinner? We could put some salmon in foil with veggies and just bake that in the oven, and I could boil some rice."

"I'm not sure I'd be that comfortable with a girls' style-your-hair night," he laughed, "but we could certainly invite Letty over for dinner. . . . Actually, I do plan to be spending more time with her, even after Muriel is laid to rest. It's a relief to me that the two of you get along so well. If we like Letty, it doesn't mean we're forgetting about Mom."

"I knew it! You have a crush on Letty, Dad!"

Amelia noticed her father's face begin flushing. She paused and then changed the subject.

"And Dad? I'm sort of beginning to like Newport."

"That's the way it happens, honey. You start to find your way around, and the charms of the place become apparent. I suspected you'd get to like it here, as I did when I was young. I was wondering what you'd think about getting a little place here of our own."

"You mean move here for good?"

"Well, aside from its view of the lighthouse, this condo has been so obviously temporary for us. At first we could think of a small house as a vacation get-away. But then, depending on the work situation, maybe we *could* make Newport our home. It's certainly been a family tradition. And we've made at least one good friend."

"And we would have ancestors right up in the cemetery, at least after tomorrow! I think I'd like to stay near Muriel. Somehow I've started to feel connected to her. And like her, I'm going back into that lighthouse, tomorrow, alone. Isn't it funny, Dad, I'm going to release her by retracing her steps."

For an instant Amelia saw that look of worry on Pah-rent's face; then he simply beamed at her.

"Penny for your thoughts," she said.

"Oh, just a dad's pride in his grown-up daughter," he replied. "Together we seem to have rediscovered our roots here on the Oregon coast. And I'm thinking that somehow time makes more sense as a circle rather than a line. Tomorrow you'll walk in the footsteps of your cousin Muriel—and now, let's have some dinner and get a good night's sleep."

28—LETTY

The appearance of Hal and Amelia at the lighthouse had been both delightful and bothersome. Usually she worked behind the scenes and had little to do with visitors to the site, but Letty had taken to these two quickly. The daughter seemed open and in need of a woman's attention. Amelia reminded Letty a little bit of herself, just in the process of growing into who she would become as a woman. Not having children of her own, Letty missed interacting with young people, and she could see herself as a sort of surrogate mother to Amelia, caring for her as she'd done for her own younger siblings at home. She didn't completely buy into the ghost story, but clearly Amelia herself believed it, and there was no harm in humoring her.

Hal . . . well, Hal was the bothersome part of the equation. Letty had to this point been extremely independent. All through college she'd avoided romantic entanglements. Her mother had all but sacrificed her own life for her children, working two jobs so that they might obtain good educations and get ahead. Letty'd lost her own father to a military accident when she was young; her role models had been the strong and determined women in her family.

And to this point, well into her satisfying career with the park service, she'd been content. But there was something about the way Hal listened to Letty, and something about his caring attention to his own daughter. It was almost as if he treated them not as a separate gender, but rather simply as people. Until, that is, the chemistry asserted itself.

Letty had felt this almost immediately, and she'd decided not to fight it. When her hand had first brushed against his, she had felt something like a jolt of electricity, which surged warmly through her body. This was a new sensation for her, and she wanted more.

Through their conversations about ghosts and bones and family trees and teen-age daughters, Letty had discovered her attraction to Hal increasing. He had a deliberate way of thinking that was grounded in strong values. Precision and responsibility were high on his list. Yet he had an openness too, and when you talked he listened so attentively that you felt like the most important person in the world.

Although he had about ten years more life experience, Letty felt she could teach him things too, and that he would willingly learn. And then there was the wonder that filled his eyes as she talked and the way that smile of delight slowly took over his entire face. Their backgrounds were so very different, yet they had each landed in Newport here and now, and it was Amelia's quest that had brought them together. Letty missed the hustle and activity of her own large family from Guadeloupe. Was it too much to hope that with this father and daughter she might begin a new circle?

She heard the door of the shed slam closed, and Letty turned from the bins to see her supervisor, Benjamin, walking toward her.

"Coffee break," he said. "Starbuck's."

A couple of times a week he'd bring her a latte and they'd catch up on her progress in the archives. Mostly he left her to her own methods in sorting the specimens and relics. He folded his tall frame into a plastic lawn chair, set down Letty's coffee, and rubbed his fingers through his short, sandy beard.

"I heard you were giving a private tour of the lighthouse yesterday," he said, with no particular tone—just an observation dropped onto the table.

"Sort of," Letty began.

How much should she tell about this development? And about the ghost business? Letty decided to tread the road of generality just to be safe.

"This man and his daughter made an appointment to talk about some ancient lighthouse history. It turns out they're related to that girl who disappeared back in 1875, and they were wondering if any remains had ever been found. Funny, we know this relative of theirs as the resident ghost, Muriel. I took the man up to the location of the iron door, and the shaft, that's all."

"I think I know who you mean. I've seen them here a few times lately. Most folks just visit once and that's it, but they've been hanging about. Let me know if they're bothering you, and I'll take care of it."

Benjamin sipped at his coffee.

Letty had followed proper protocols in relinquishing the bone fragment to certified kin, and she'd registered and filed that transaction appropriately. As for tomorrow's ritual, well, that would harm no one and nothing as far as she could anticipate. She made a snap decision not to tell her boss the backstory, and with that decision she threw her allegiance to Hal and Amelia. The ritual would remain a secret among the three of them, and Letty felt good with that sense of intimacy. It bound them together.

"Oh, no, no bother at all," she assured her boss. "They're nice people—the man's old Newport and a marine biologist, and the girl is sweet—fretting about her ancient cousin and the apparent tragedy that befell her. It's been sort of fun sharing lighthouse history with interested parties."

"We're here to serve as we may," Benjamin said with a smile and gulped down the last of his coffee before he extricated himself from the small plastic chair. "Just as long as they're not ghost-hunters," he chuckled half under his breath as he headed out the door.

Letty's heart quickened as she turned to log in her hours on the work-schedule chart, clearly marking 9 a.m. for tomorrow. She made an additional note: "work away from office."

29—Amelia

D-day had finally arrived—or as she mentally termed it, R-day, release day for Muriel. Amelia had slept fitfully. Several times she had risen to peer out into the blackness toward the light-house, and sure enough, the third time, toward morning, she thought she had seen a faint light in the tower.

She could hear Pah-rent in the kitchen. Amelia laid out her jeans and shirt on the bed, then dug in her pack for the spirit-spray, which she applied thoroughly to her clothes, noting no detectable odor. She sprayed a spurt onto her sneakers, too, and as an afterthought, she spritzed the baggie containing Muriel's bone. As she got dressed Amelia rehearsed the lines that Fatima had told her. First was the "I mean you no harm" speech and then the brief prayer. They were both short and to the point, and even if she didn't have Fatima's exact words, Amelia was sure she could recite the gist of the ritual's incantation. She was anxious to begin her dutiful act.

She felt confident about what needed to be done, yet she was glad that Pah-rent would be outside in the car, and Letty too. If she truly was to become the transport vessel for Muriel's spirit, there were many unknowns about how this might affect Amelia herself. She was pretty sure that Muriel's spirit was not evil, but the process seemed unusual and sort of risky.

Amelia wished she could discuss her concerns—she almost thought "qualms"—with Pah-rent. But Fatima had cautioned her to secrecy, and the uncertainties were nagging at her. What would happen to Amelia's own personality when she breathed in Muriel's spirit? Might Muriel's ghost—so long without a material body—be tempted to take Amelia over? In theory getting her to the cemetery sounded simple, but Amelia feared she might lose herself in the process, or be forever changed. Following through on what was turning into a heroic feat was the biggest challenge she had ever faced, and of necessity she had to perform it solo.

She had considered backing out. After all, who was she answerable to? Releasing Muriel from the lighthouse was a choice Amelia herself had made, and the decision to act had been based more on an empathetic feeling than on any actual logic. She could imagine herself in Muriel's situation, and the helplessness was overwhelming. Amelia felt an obligation to help as she could. This was beyond even a life-and-death situation. And then, Muriel was her ancestor and so much like herself, bereft of her mother.

Lucky that Amelia, a receptive cousin, had chanced upon the lighthouse. Lucky that they'd seen the candleglow from the condo window, and lucky that Amelia'd found the book with Muriel's story. Fortunate too, that they'd seen Muriel materialize—and definitely felt the chill of her presence.

Really, the circumstances had already decided for Amelia. This was a task she must accomplish—potential dangers aside—and she must simply grow up and do it alone. She tried to think of comparable moments in her life up to now. The hardest thing had been going on after Mom died. Mom's death had made Amelia face something she could not fix or change. And it had made her ponder for the first time what happened to people when they left the world of the living. Amelia wanted to think that somehow a person never was totally obliterated. She knew she still carried Mom inside her. Sometimes she could almost hear her voice in her head comforting her, giving her good advice.

Amelia had seen Muriel's face, but she'd felt Muriel's personality too. Something about her distant cousin from so long ago lived vividly on, and clearly she needed help from someone who still walked this earth.

Amelia went over her two speeches one last time and gathered up her backpack. Pah-rent wasn't in the kitchen now; he was sitting in the chair near the window, staring at the lighthouse.

"Dad." Hal jumped with surprise at hearing her voice. "Is the cross ready?"

"In the car, honey. Is it time? I've got the shovel in the trunk."

They settled into their seats for the short drive across the bridge, sitting together in solemn silence.

"You're sure you want to go through with this?" Pah-rent asked as he drove to the back of the lighthouse near the shed.

"I have to, Dad."

Letty came out of the shed and waved at them. Amelia pulled the bone out of her backpack, and when they got out of the car Dad hugged her hard.

"We'll be right here," he assured her. "And if you're not back in fifteen minutes, I'm coming in there."

Amelia smiled. "I'll be all right. Just be ready to drive to the cemetery."

Amelia stepped into the lighthouse by way of the kitchen door. She walked straight ahead into the dining room, where the registration desk was not yet staffed. She turned left and stood just inside the front door, facing the solid staircase. For an instant her instinct was to turn on her heel and retrace her path back out the kitchen door. Only she would know what had transpired here in the lighthouse. She could even pretend she was carrying Muriel's ghost and go through an entire charade of laying her to rest, with no risk or danger to herself in the process. Who would know the difference? –Well, except for herself and Muriel.

Bone-bag in hand, Amelia steeled herself and climbed the straight flight ahead of her with resolve, stepped quickly across the landing, and began to mount the thirteen steps in the spiral leading to the place of the iron door—and the ghost of Muriel. The lighthouse was gloomily dark and deathly still. Amelia's heart pounded.

She stood in front of the spot where Muriel's handkerchief—and her blood—had been found by Harold all those decades ago. The air felt calm and warm. Amelia held out the baggie and unzipped its seal, just in case somehow it needed to send out its essence to attract the ghost. Amelia cleared her throat.

"Muriel? I mean you no harm," she said softly. "Come into me. I hold forth your earthly remains. I will be your vessel and take you to rest."

Amelia's arms were quivering as she held out the bone, but she closed her eyes and thought of the face she'd seen in the window, the face she'd drawn in her sketchbook. She mentally bathed that image in clear, bright light. When she could hold the image steady and strong, she began the breaths, three short exhalations, then a deep breath in, down to the core of her own being. This calmed her, and she repeated the sequence twice—making sure not to exceed a total of three. In the second sequence she thought she felt a chill in the air, like icy fingers grasping at her. She intensified her focus, resisting the chill. Her eyes slitted open for a second, retaining the image of Muriel's face Amelia held in her mind. Or was the face truly hovering there right before her on the landing? On the third deep inhalation, Amelia's chest felt something like tremors. Her insides seemed to be repositioning, moving from side to side. A brief wave of nausea overtook her, but Amelia swallowed and pushed it down. The upper landing began to spin around her.

Amelia was sure that the ritual had worked. Muriel was with her, but Amelia wasn't certain her own being could handle this extra spirit. She felt woozy and disoriented. Could she even make it down the stairs and back out to the safety of Pah-rent and Letty and the car? She closed her eyes to steady the spinning, and unfamiliar images began to flit before her, as if she was seeing the world through Muriel's point of view: men in hats and women with long skirts, horse-drawn wagons, muddy streets leading to the familiar bay and rolling surf of the shore. She opened her eyes only to find these antiquated visions replaced with an awareness of other spirits with her right there in the lighthouse, pale images of faces with faraway looks in their own eyes.

Amelia guided herself down the spiral stairs by extending her arms to the walls on both sides. From the landing she could see a man floating up the main staircase toward her and a long-skirted woman passing by in the hallway below.

A voice in her head commanded her, "Walk down the stairs. Brush past the ghostly gentleman. He will pay you no notice."

After placing one foot carefully on each step, Amelia found herself facing the front door. Almost like an automaton, she pivoted right and right again, heading for the kitchen door in the back. The handle miraculously yielded to her touch, and she deliberately strode toward the metal wagon near the shed, with the man and woman leaning against it. They stopped their conversation and looked up at her expectantly.

"There you are, honey! Job all taken care of?" the man asked.

With a reedy voice vibrating with a doubled undertone, she replied, "Take us to the graveyard."

30—Amelia and Muriel

"I hope that cross isn't in your way," the man said over his shoulder. The woman turned her head from the passenger seat in front to check on Amelia, who was wedged into the back seat with the rustic cross. Amelia was staring blankly out the side window.

"I'm probably not supposed to ask, according to Madame Fatima's orders, but how did your ritual go in there? Did you make contact with Muriel?" the man continued. He shot a quick smile toward the passenger seat.

Upon hearing the name *Muriel*, Amelia startled to attention. She looked forward, and her eyes moved slowly from the man to the woman and back again.

"Yes, here we are," she finally responded, still in that strange and deliberate reedy tone. "It's awfully bright. And this metal wagon moves so quickly, even without horses."

The man glanced quickly toward the woman.

"Amelia, honey, are you all right?"

"Is this the way to the graveyard?" she replied, again moving her head to look out the window. "I recognize nothing."

"Don't you remember? This is the way we came before. Rte. 20 and then up the hill at Third."

"Is it a far journey?"

"No—we'll be there in a couple of minutes, silly."

As they moved up Yaquina Heights, they slowed over a curve next to a field containing three horses and two alpacas.

Amelia stared and then muttered, "Such strange beasts among the steeds."

"What's that, Amelia?" the man asked. Amelia blinked as if against the bright light.

"What, Dad? I didn't say anything."

She felt strange, almost ill. As she looked out the window her vision seemed to blur, blending things as she knew them with another, more primitive view. And even her thinking seemed affected. A different voice, with a different vocabulary, seemed to want to speak inside her head. She realized that this must be Muriel—that Fatima's ritual had actually worked and she was carrying the spirit of her ancient cousin within her own being.

It was a frightening sensation. At moments Amelia's own self seemed to disappear, and Muriel took over. Amelia had no means of controlling this change or of asserting herself. As they neared the graveyard she wondered if Muriel would be willing to be laid to rest. Had Amelia unwittingly put her own future in danger? Would she now have to endure an unsettling double life? She knew Muriel's spirit was not evil, but she felt inside her a life that wanted to go on living, a life that was excited about being liberated from its confinement in the lighthouse.

Dad pulled the car in next to the caretaker's shack, and he and Letty got out. He stuck his head back inside the car, and she recognized that concerned look on his face.

"Can't you tell us what went on back there in the lighthouse?" he asked. "Did something happen to you? You seem funny, and kind of sick," he observed. "Are you well enough to follow through on this? Maybe we should just go on back to the condo. The entire prospect of this ritual has just got you overexcited, I think. Maybe sort of giddy."

She tried to smile and give him a reassuring look, all the while struggling against a rising Muriel, who seemed even stronger now that they had arrived at the cemetery.

"I'm okay, Dad. Let's go on with it. We have the cross—and Muriel is relying on us."

He opened the back car door and began maneuvering out the clumsy cross. Letty opened the opposite door and extracted Amelia. She looked around with wonder.

"Letty, can you carry the shovel?" Hal asked from behind the open trunk. "Lucky for us, I don't think anyone's on duty today. This cross is cumbersome to manage. Amelia, you have the baggie with the bone, right?"

She joined him at the trunk, with very round eyes, holding out the baggie reverently. Letty took the shovel in one hand and Amelia's arm in the other.

"Lead the way, will you?" she said to him. "Amelia seems sort of overwhelmed by all this."

They crossed the narrow road and stepped up a short embankment. Hal headed toward the tree-of-many-trunks, winding his way among the scattered headstones. Letty followed, guiding Amelia, who was reading the names and dates as they passed each marker. Hal was getting quite a lead on them.

"C'mon, honey," Letty urged.

Hal stopped and looked back toward them.

"It's easy to get disoriented," he called out. "But I've located him. Here's Harold, Amelia, just where he was before."

Amelia froze in her tracks.

"Harold?" she said to Letty, looking her directly in the eyes. "He's here?"

"Your dad's found his plot," Letty replied as she exerted pressure on Amelia's arm to propel her forward.

They joined Hal at Harold's grave. Amelia immediately knelt down and traced her fingers across the raised letters of his name on the stone.

Hal set down the cross, took the shovel from Letty, and began to dig a shallow hole nearby. Letty joined him to offer advice and encouragement. Amelia heard their soft voices as if coming to her through a fog.

"Oof, the ground's full of roots," he commented, "but once I get past the surface layer it should go quickly. Maybe just a foot deep will do it, to protect the bone and set in the cross."

"Amelia seems stunned now that we're actually performing the ritual," Letty confided in a low voice. "Wasn't she acting strange in the car? Sort of distant? I hope we're doing the right thing."

"I know my daughter," said Hal quietly as he paused to rest on his shovel. "Once she's set her mind on something, there's no stopping her. She even used to have struggles of will with her mother. . . . I'm sure glad other folks have planted bushes up here," he said as he resumed digging. "I feel like a prankster, digging around in a cemetery. . . . There, that should be deep enough. . . . Amelia, bring the baggie!" he said in a loud voice.

Letty and Hal turned back to Harold's grave. At first, it seemed that Amelia had disappeared, but in the dappled light they saw her, lying on her back in front of Harold's stone.

"Sweetheart, we need you here," he called to her.

She continued to stare at the sky. For the moment Muriel had overcome Amelia, and the girl from the past was reading the modern girl's mind.

Amelia's feelings over the last half year washed over Muriel, who began to feel an even stronger kinship with her modern counterpart. Muriel felt the joyful attention the girl received from her mother and the horror of her diagnosis, then the sad quiet time as the mother dwindled away, only to join the ranks of the dead—so different from her own wrenching away from her mother yet equally as earth-shaking. She saw the focused concern of Amelia's father and felt the warmth of his protective love. It touched her so deeply that she herself felt an unaccustomed warmth, remembering the care of her own father—and that longing for his return. She saw that Amelia had romantic desires, and she recalled the thrill of Harold's attentions.

As these feelings passed through her consciousness like images projected on a screen, Muriel experienced for a moment a resistance to accepting her final interment. Painful as life was, and had been for her, something in her wanted to go on, to try it still—or again.

Hal gave an alarmed look at Letty and strode over to what he thought was his daughter. Kneeling down, he touched her arm.

"Amelia," he said softly, then louder.

"This is the place," she intoned in that reedy voice.

"Yes," he said as he shook her slightly, "this is the place to put Muriel to rest."

She felt a slow, almost reluctant change pass over her vision, and she moved her gaze to his face.

"Dad?"

"Come on, Amelia. The hole is ready for the bone. Say your words, and we'll put up the cross."

He extended his hand and pulled Amelia to her feet. She picked up the baggie and followed him to Letty and the newly-dug hole.

She now clearly recalled her mission. She was herself again.

"Um, could you stand over there?"

Amelia pointed to a stone bench several feet away. Her voice regained its girlish tone.

"Fatima said I must do this alone." She was banking on the last part of the ritual releasing her from this doubleness, and she needed a clear focus to perform it properly.

They watched from a distance as Amelia bent down and carefully situated the baggie in the hole. She picked up the shovel and replaced the loose dirt, burying the bone but leaving a spot to insert the cross. She said something softly that could not be overheard. Amelia bowed her head then lifted it up again, raised her arms, and breathed in and out deeply. The leaves above rustled gently, and Amelia felt relieved of an enormous heaviness that had burdened her down. She turned toward Hal and Letty and gestured them forward.

"Dad? Can you put up the cross?"

He inserted the cross into the small indentation and Letty steadied it while he filled the hole completely and tamped down the dirt.

Amelia watched, then said with authority, "Now will you say with me, 'God keep you in eternal peace'? It's a prayer for Muriel."

The three of them joined hands, and Amelia began.

Together they said the prayer aloud, and it echoed back to them from the leaf canopy: "God keep you in eternal peace."

They walked in solemn silence under the tall trees back to the car. Amelia knew she had been through an experience that no one could quite explain but that had brought her into the grown-up world and altered her outlook. She felt both happy and sad, relieved and regretful. The entire ritual was really the funeral Muriel had never had. It was fitting that they were the ones laying her to rest, as her only remaining family.

Amelia ran what she knew of the details of Muriel's life over in her mind, and it was a sad tale.

The adoration of Harold was, Amelia hoped, a high point for her cousin, and there was the happiness that somehow in their deaths and their afterlife, whatever that was like, they would be near each other. Amelia felt relieved of the burden of her obligation and of the weighty soul that for a brief while accompanied her own, yet she regretted that she and Muriel had not actually conversed. She had glimpsed the world through Muriel's being, yet who could fully know the heart of another?

As he put the shovel in the trunk, Dad broke the silence: "Honey, I'm proud of you. This was your mission, and well, not to be corny, but 'mission accomplished!'"

He put his hands on his hips and faced her.

Amelia smiled warmly as Letty looked on. She could not even begin to tell him about the change to her outlook that had occurred. For a while this would be her secret treasure, that for a few minutes another life combined with hers, and she had seen the world around her through a different lens. Muriel's spirit might well be successfully relocated to her proper resting place, but the trace of her remained within Amelia. She could still feel her presence.

The thoughts crowded into Amelia's mind, how grateful she was for her loving father. She was learning how you never really left the past behind, how your ancestors and your loved ones found homes within your own soul. And this is why your actions mattered, for you were answerable to a whole line of people before you who also had struggled and striven, loved and lost.

Dad reached into his pocket and pulled out Amelia's confiscated cell phone, which she hadn't seen for nearly a month. Lately she hadn't even missed it.

As he extended it toward her, he said, "I think you've earned this reward."

"No, you keep it," Amelia replied without hesitation. "I won't be needing it."

She reached out her arms to pull both her father and Letty into a grand circular embrace.

EPILOGUE

As she pushed the stroller along the path of the south jetty, Amelia, now a young mother, looked over at the lighthouse with its placid eyes staring out at the bay. She hadn't visited Newport since her marriage to Tom, and being here again had put her in a contemplative mood. She'd walked up the stairs to the lighthouse yesterday, remembering the vision of Muriel's face behind her at the window all those years ago. She hoped Muriel was resting in peace. Inside the lighthouse, and even up toward the place of the iron door now completely cordoned off, Amelia felt no ghostly presence. Of course she knew, from those moments when she had seen through Muriel's eyes, that other spirits still floated aimlessly, harmlessly, through the house. She was relieved that they no longer appeared before her own eyes. Yet it did remind her that we don't always see everything that might be present before us.

Hal bent down to replace the "plug" in the fussing baby's mouth. Amelia and Tom had named her Ariel, after Prospero's airy spirit in *The Tempest*, but it also combined the words Amelia and Muriel into one. No one else, not even Amelia's husband, could ever know how appropriate that was. Of course Amelia'd told Tom about her rescue of the ghost, yet no telling could capture that merging of the two selves in a single body.

"There's our lighthouse, looking just the way it did from our condo that summer," Dad commented as he stood. "But now there's no feeble light sending out its cry for help at night, thanks to your efforts. Unless, of course, another trapped soul replaced dear Muriel."

"Have you seen another ghost?" Amelia asked. "You were the first to spot Muriel, after all."

"No, no," Hal laughed. "Actually, while I'm aware of its presence daily, I don't visit the place anymore. It's become just part of the landscape."

"I can hardly look up at the bridge without imagining the image of you laboring over with that cross on your back," Amelia reminisced. "Remember that first day we saw the tall ship? It just came out of the mist like something magical. And what a strange coincidence, that Muriel's mother had been shanghaied by pirates. It was an omen that we would find her, I think, and help with her release."

"It's always good to look back on our life paths and see the patterns and connections," Dad observed. "But the cause-and-effect isn't always so clear. I suppose you could say that it was because of Muriel I found Letty and moved back to Newport. Or that it was Muriel who helped you become the brave and independent mother you are today. And look at us—we're talking about the effect of someone who never actually existed in our time, as if she were real."

"She was real to me, Dad. And I've discovered a little part of her in myself still to this day. She helped make me who I am. . . . I have never directly thanked you, Dad, for trusting me and my mission all those years ago. Both you and Muriel helped to teach me two things, at least: people have to look out for each other, and each of us comes from a long line of family. Our lives reach backward and forward at the same time. Look at us three today—grandfather, mother, child—we're the perfect image of what I'm talking about."

Hal stretched out his hand to his daughter, and they joined together to walk behind the stroller, both helping to push it along. Occasionally they'd spot a seal raising its head out of the sparkling waters of the bay. It was a perfect day.

"Can you watch Ariel for me awhile?" Amelia finally broke the calm silence. "There's an errand I need to do—by myself."

They returned to her car, and she dropped her father and daughter off at their bungalow just above Agate Beach. Amelia made her way up Rte. 20 to the cemetery turn-off. She was nearly on auto-pilot. This seemed like familiar home territory.

After the curves Amelia turned into the Eureka Cemetery and parked near the caretaker's shed as they'd done that day she carried Muriel's spirit within her—that day that had changed her forever. She stepped up the embankment and spotted the tree-of-many-trunks, still lush with its twists and turns. She could probably have found Harold's grave even in her sleep, but today it was the small rustic cross that caught her eye and guided her directly to the resting place of the two lovers.

The cross was weathered now. Amelia took several deep breaths and felt a communion with her distant ancestor. How strange that she, like Muriel, had found her true love at an early age, and now they too were together, like Harold and Muriel but above ground. As on that day years ago she repeated the prayer that Fatima had taught her: "Muriel, may God keep you in his eternal peace." Amelia lay down her bag and tugged a few stray clumps of grass away from Harold's marker. She turned to look at the horizon far west, where the blue of the ocean met the blue of the sky with only the faintest line of demarcation between them.

It was serenely peaceful here. Amelia also felt at peace and hoped that when her own days on earth were done she too might find such a tranquil spot for a grave—and that she might be surrounded by her own family.

As she stooped to pick up her bag, she saw a colorful piece of wrapping paper peeking from its side pocket. Curious, she tugged at it and pulled out a small, soft package tied with a yellow ribbon. Its tiny card was slipped just under a lop-sided bow. Amelia opened it and read "For my forever lover, best mother of our precious daughter. I'm waiting for your return. I love you with all my being, Tom."

With a tear forming at the corner of her eye, she opened the package, thinking how grateful she was that transporting Muriel here to the graveyard had not endangered Amelia's own life, or her spirit. It was Dad, and Tom, and Ariel, and even Letty who gave meaning to her life. What would she do if she'd lost any of them? *You would light your candle as a beacon every night, for decades if that's what was required,* a voice said in her head. *Faith must persist and love will endure.*

Amelia smiled and shook her head slightly to shrug off that voice, surely Muriel's, that spoke within her from time to time. She did not feel threatened by its presence. The messages served to remind her of the fragility of life and the preciousness of our time on earth together. The wisdom of Muriel's vision enriched Amelia every day.

The paper fell off the small package, revealing a finely-made lace handkerchief embroidered with strawberries. Amelia's heart lurched for an instant: it resembled in her imagination Muriel's own that had been stained with drops of her blood. How could Tom have known that? Did he mean this as some kind of joke? Surely her husband had no such similarity in mind, she told herself as her heart slowed back down. Surely Tom meant it only as a sweet token of his love. And so she would consider it, in the spirit of its giving.

Amelia stuffed the wrapping and ribbon back into her bag and held the love-token in her hand as she turned toward the care-taker's shed. The gift gave her strength and made her eager to return to her family.

What Amelia did not notice as she pivoted to walk back to the car was that the handkerchief slipped from her hand. A gust of wind caught it, and it fluttered in the wind, finally resting on the earth directly between the graves of the two lovers. And the cross shifted suddenly—jolting just slightly to the left—as if the earth had settled a bit at that very instant.

Acknowledgments

I'd like to thank all the people who showed enthusiasm for this project and offered their support along the way. First, I garnered inspiration from the lighthouse itself and from Lischen M. Miller's story of the ghost. Mariah Matthews' Focus Group encouraged me to continue this novel, and especially Margaret Arvanitis, who read it in complete manuscript. I would be nowhere without Ruth F. Harrison's Tuesday Writers of Waldport, who kept my characters true and helped me be more expansive when I was too eager to hurry through episodes. Brenda Croghan, Shirley Plummer, Aron Rothstein, and Dan Taber were my first, best readers. Donny King accompanied me on field work research with good humor and good will and patience. And Newport herself, with her grand art deco bridge and picturesque historical sites, loomed perpetually in my creative imagination. I especially want to thank the Lincoln County Historical Society for accepting my argument that history comes alive in literature.

Made in the USA
Coppell, TX
18 November 2023

24431857R00095